1

Peter Kent

The Legend of the Stones of Life

(The birth of the Gods)

To the memory of my beloved mom Mária

(1952 – 2011)

ILLUSTRATIONS: AI Microsoft

ENGLISH TRANSLATION: Martina Milner

The Legend of the Stones of Life

(The birth of the Gods)

Prologue

Autotrophic living organisms are organisms obtaining their energy from the sunlight using photosynthesis.

Heterotrophic living organisms are organisms deriving their intake of nutrition from other living organisms, which are their source of food.

I am on a beautiful beach, watching our lovely star rising above the horizon. I am listening to the soothing sound of the sea and the gentle rays of the rising star are touching my face. I breathe in this fresh air, my whole body is being washed by the sea breeze, leaving the goosebumps on my skin. When I look at the sky, it is already crystal clear and blue, as if mirrored with the sea. Our world, almost untouched by any other creatures, is a real beauty. I can see our cities in the air, we call them arkols. They look like huge tears in the sky, lined by the clouds which are being carried away by the wind and they are calmly following their path.

My name is Jaz Tar Akesiun. Together with my love Ites Era Lamesian, who has been chosen for me by the destiny itself, we are the governors of the world of Asnium. Now you are probably asking yourselves who I am. I come from the world utterly different from yours, my dear humans. I am sending you a message, you extraordinary creatures, characterized by the shape and diversity of your kind. It is mostly about your personality. We have been watching you for ages, your rich history and especially the nature and development of your thinking. You can like and dislike, you are capable of both love and hatred, you can be united but also selfish, generous, and yet greedy and mean. And I could go on and on and make an exceptionally long list of the characteristics of your nature. We are unable to figure you out, we are not sure whether you could be our friends or our enemies. We are peaceful beings although it sometimes wouldn't seem so. We are exceedingly rare race in the universe. We are autotrophic organisms, and we obtain our energy from the sun and additionally from the water. We are related to plants, but unlike plants, we are humanoid, moving and thinking beings representing an exceptional living structure in the universe. We are very tall, about one and half times taller than you - people. Our skin is very taut and springy, and it resembles a snakeskin a bit. Some of us have a gold and green complexion, the others are silver or a little purple or light brown... And so, I could carry on naming our races. Our faces are beautifully developed, just as yours. However, we don't put on much fat. We enjoy doing sports and our bodies are athletic and we like having fun just as you do. Therefore, I am going to tell you our story, the story of our creation, I am going to tell you about the type of our nature and our diverse history.

I am trying to find the right words to explain our similarities. What we surely do have in common is our passionate eagerness for knowledge and information that could clarify the creation of our existence. It remains a mystery and we also only rely on our legends and rumors. However, some parts of our history are still alive and that's why we are somewhere else when it comes to knowledge. We are one of the ancient civilizations in the universe, which you know in your visible spectre. The outer space is quite varied. You will never see us. Or perhaps you will if you detect this signal which consists of the thoughts, I am sending you. We also possess telepathic abilities, but we only use them at very long distances in the space. Generally, we communicate verbally, just as you do. We have some unique technologies that make our lives much easier. You obviously can't understand this, but it doesn't matter. It is important that one day in the future you will detect our signal and your improved consciousness will enable you to understand how fragile life in the universe is, you will learn to appreciate and protect it, look after it and help develop it. Because this is also our aim, the aim of Asnians. I truly believe that you will find the story of the creation of our ancient civilization in the universe interesting.

First of all, I am going to tell you about the current inhabitants of the kingdom of Asnium, about our technologies, government and life. Unlike you, people, we are autotrophic living beings. We don't need to eat and spend time hunting other living creatures. We live on pure water and the sunlight from our star. Our bodies can adapt to any gravitation, we are literally born for space flights. Furthermore, our mind and largely extended consciousness can slowly and gradually form our bodies. We find material things worthless. We prefer the value of knowledge. Information is priceless, everything else only has a utility value. We are like migratory birds; we have survived several deaths of the stars.

There are two types of beings, one that destroys, the other that creates. The beings that go for destruction must consider that one day they will also destroy themselves. On the other hand, the beings that create may bloom in the beauty. They may be transformed thanks to social and omnipotent love into the rich, flourishing, and colorful infinite world. This is the only way how to rule the universe. You may become Gods and develop the universe using the technologies that create, not those that destroy. And here we are coming closer to the story of the creation of our civilization, to the story of how our legend was born. You have your own legends about the creation of your civilization on your planet, too.

At first, let me tell you about our civilization and how we live.

Rule wisely, put all your heart and love in it and your nation will love you as much as you love your nation.

The government of three planets Akretium, Balium and Cesnium is the global government of three planets consisting of the Council of Elders which has ten thousand members and two government administrators. There are ten thousand of them because it is a magical border at which it can be seen whether an individual is immortal or an ordinary mortal. And there is also a spiritual nature. Asnians are divided into five categories of beings with different life expectancy. The first and the biggest category amounts to the living beings with the lowest life expectancy, they live to one hundred and twenty years. They are like an autotrophic version of you. However, their bodies are a bit firmer and when it comes to the ability to survive, they are more adaptable, and they have many useful skills. They make 55% of the population on our planets. The beings in the second category live to between one hundred and twenty to five hundred years. They are not so different from the short-lived, but their bodies are even firmer, and they are more adaptable to the changing conditions and their wounds heal faster. This category represents about 25% of the inhabitants of our planets.

The beings in the third category live to a relatively old age, almost one thousand years and they hold remarkably high and important positions in the society. They make almost 10% of the population on our planets. They are heterotrophic living beings, just like those in the fourth category, but finally they will not escape the cruel death. They are stronger and much more adaptive, they eat plants, and they are Admans, so called protectors, and they live mostly in the admikols in the space environment.

Then there is the fourth – immensely powerful – category of beings that live to ten thousand years. They make 9% of the population. Their bodies are extraordinarily strong, they are taller than the others and some of them are in our army, but they may also work in some of our industries. A lot of them may be found in the Council of Elders. Their injuries heal amazingly fast, and their limbs can regenerate very quickly, too.

The fifth category is the smallest one and it is where I belong as well. We are immortal, or better said, relatively immortal. Immortal in the living organic environment. It is impossible to say how old we are because our bodies adapt to the different conditions very well. We are more mature than the rest of the inhabitants in the kingdom. We started assumed power about three hundred million years ago and we established the new order based on mutual respect and love. Honestly, being immortal is a curse, it brings great misery and grief each time we lose our close friends and members of our family, so we decided to create our own world that nobody else knows about. Even its location in the universe is only known to the immortals who already live there. Just a handful of the immortals are born, they don't even make one per cent of the population of our kingdom. Moreover, king Arbatron, who was the very first immortal, has been our king since forever and it was him who gave our kingdom its name – Asnium.

King Arbatron is famous for keeping one tradition – he comes to visit his kingdom every ten thousand years. His visit is a big celebration, and everybody enjoys it dearly. He is loved by all of us because he is the king who terminated all conflicts, quarrels, hatred, and envy among the inhabitants on these planets. He set up the Order of the Council of Elders and simplified the laws. We don't have many of them and they are clear and accurate and easy to understand. Since then, we have lived in peace and welfare which no one even dreamt of. Our king is exceedingly kind, but he can also be very strict when his rules are broken. However, it hasn't happened for a long time. And when he is leaving, he takes a few of newly born immortals with him and he appoints two administrators of the government who have been elected and passed the trials of skill. This way he makes sure that the government and the administration keep working properly. Asnians sometimes call the immortals the prophets because nobody else has their abilities. However, the immortals don't interfere with the work of the government. Yet they have the power to intervene if the situation that has arisen somehow threatens the progress of life in infinite love and welfare and respect for one another. They represent a kind of supervision of the government of Asnium. Asnians and the others who belong to the Asnian government become its members when they are nine thousand years old, and they are elected for the period of one thousand years. This government of the Council of Elders, some beings call it also the Council of Sages, is responsible for maintaining the lasting peace, stability, and welfare on all three planets. They take care of the education of the other rulers – the creators, who build up other civilizations and ensure the development of life in the universe, too. These are then subject to the global government of three planets, whose centre is the planet of Akretium.

Planet Akretium and its capital city of Milidrium. Milidrium is where The Council of Sages is based. It is the largest arkol, also called the city of palaces and huge cathedrals. The biggest one of them is the headquarters of the government and the sages meet there regularly. It is impressive and shiny, and it has white and silver color. It is the gem of our whole civilization. Throughout the ages, a lot of governments of those wisest entities worked on it and helped to build it. All sages, those ten thousand brave ones, live here in the palaces inside this magnificent arkol. I wish you could see it. You'd be stunned and just ask yourselves: What gardens of Eden are they?

Let's talk about those ten thousand brave ones. They are divided into two groups: five thousand women represented by an immortal female administrator elected for ten thousand years and five thousand men represented by an immortal male administrator elected for ten thousand years. These two representatives make a new couple and Asnians say that it is a match made in heaven. These two administrators have to fulfil all requirements necessary for the administration, they need to go through all seven grades in the school centres, just like the sages. It is essential that they have been on a lot of journeys through the space, and they have made a significant contribution to the development of life. We are a sort of painters; we can create the stars. Entities may choose whether they will destroy or create. We create and so we have become Gods in the universe although we hardly ever consider ourselves as Gods.

Regarding the administration – it is crucial that you understand that the administrators need to be elected and they have to pass the trials of skill, just like everyone who is the member of the Council of Sages. Furthermore, these two administrators have to agree that they will live in a partnership and their trials of skill are different from those of applicants for a standard seat in the Council. Both administrators have to accept these conditions. Whether they belong together or not will be finally revealed after these trials therefore they are more difficult that the usual ones. (Sometimes the individuals don't pass the trials.) This rule comes out of the belief that if one is to govern with love, peace and understanding, it has to be real love of a couple matched in heaven. That is why the Asnian government is not actually a government, it is more like an administration responsible for lives and development of all entities living on these three planets. It is a real honor to serve the inhabitants. This opportunity arises when, for example, one of the members of the Council is about to be more than ten thousand years old and they need to resign and free their seat to somebody who is going to be nine thousand years old. Each seat, including the administrator's one, may be connected to the destiny in a way. Therefore, Asnians sometimes call them the seats of destiny. If the most prestigious mission is granted to an Asnian, it has been destined to be so. It simply can't be a coincidence. All applicants who have accepted the challenge to become the members of the government need to take part in a three-month campaign during which they visit all three planets, and they are attempting to win the support of the majority of inhabitants.

Those who get the most votes in the elections will fight for a seat in the final battle. They need to prove they are worth it. This battle lasts seven weeks and the applicants have to pass the trials of skill organized by a member who is leaving the Council and giving up his seat, by each of the ten thousand present ones and last but not least king Arbatron, who then appoints the administrators for the period of ten thousand years until he comes back for them. Everybody who gets into the Council of Sages has seven weeks to prove that they are able to implement their visions, which helped them to win the support of the inhabitants of all three planets, into practical life in the name of love, peace and global welfare. This final test is the most complex and hardest of all because it is difficult to replace the one who is resigning and who makes sure that the test is genuinely harsh. The new applicant needs to be as capable as their predecessor, if not even better. They are flooded with questions that are not easy to answer. However, the truly versed and tenacious applicant will not be discouraged by anything. And to make matters worse, they put them into a variety of situations, and they must come up with the solutions. They need to be very prompt; they experience serious mental distress and are under time pressure. That is why not just anyone can become a member of this government. Furthermore, in addition to the knowledge, mental and spiritual aspects, they must also be physically fit. Therefore, they need to pass the tests of physical condition too. This is particularly important, because to rule three worlds is also about overall physical, mental, and spiritual health.

So, this is how it works. Sometimes certain individuals fail the trials despite having been elected by the masses. When it happens, it is all right. We do not judge anyone here. Nobody is perfect, not even us, Asnias. Yes, we are also adorned with imperfections, and we make mistakes, but we take it easy, we rise up and learn our lessons, we move on and we try to put things right again with the proper reactions and acts. After all, that is what our life is about. About the tests and trials which make us better, stronger, and happier because we are learning something new. If there were no mistakes, what would our life be like? Most likely very boring and nobody in the whole universe or on our three planets wants that. Asnians love having fun. The individual who fails the trials of skill will not get the second chance to do them, but they are automatically rewarded with other important position. This rule is immutable, and the position cannot be refused. They can choose any training centre on one of the planets and become its administrators for one hundred years. Their task is to prepare our future generations for various difficult situations of a spiritual, mental, and physical nature. There is a good reason for this rule. Asnians have learnt that even negative experience can be very instructive for the future generations. Therefore, even these unsuccessful pilgrims are very important in the hierarchy of Asnians, whose mission does not only need to be to rule, but also to teach the future generations how to be proficient in all the trials that life will bring. Everything is related to everything else.

Our law, politics and philosophy are built on different moral and social traditions. Before we get to talk about our philosophy, let's answer the following question: Who is governed by the Council of Sages? I am going to introduce them to you. Our society consists of several ethnic groups, but there are a few basic ones.

Moranians are thought to be the very first inhabitants, the very first living and intelligent form that was ever born. They are amphibians. They don't have hair and their skin is similar to that of a snake. They are mostly gold and green color, and their size depends on how long they live. They have gills in the chest area and have very well-developed swimming membranes among the toes. Their nostrils are less developed, they look like two tiny holes. Their mouths are slightly smaller than usual and look more like huge scars on their heads.

Admans are the first extraplanetary living form that emerged. They are medium tall, from one hundred eighty to one hundred ninety centimeters and they almost resemble people, but they are more adaptive to adverse conditions. Their wounds heal better, and their limbs can regenerate but they can be fatally injured.

Akretans represent an advanced form of life from which the first immortal individual arose, and they were the first who were able to establish the long-term peace. They are lovely and very tall, with beautiful faces. They are athletic and their skin of mostly white and silver color is very firm.

Balians come from the second planet of Balium. They live to a middle age, but they are autotrophic entities of mostly medium-tall stature. Their light brown colour makes them very exceptional creatures with slightly firmer bodies.

Cesnians are a blend of living forms. We can see them as an artificially made form of life which was finally able to develop itself and colonize the planet of Cesnium. This planet is not one of those most hospitable ones, but the Cesnians proved to be the strong living form which may still evolve. They are used in the army as a backup to protect the entire kingdom of Asnium. They are autotrophic entities; their skin is mostly light white. Their bodies are even firmer.

Kateitans are an incredibly old civilization living a bit differently. They are a kind of monks living in the monasteries and they do nothing but meditate and they are devoted to the spiritual life. It is a particularly useful form of life because they lead us on the path to discovering the greatest mysteries that go beyond the cosmic ones.

Xieratians are great biologists. They helped king Arbatron to become immortal. However, they cannot explain how they managed to do it; this knowledge is still a great mystery. The fact is that a handful of the inhabitants just can become immortal.

And then there are Nardians, who are a bit like Morans, but they were born on the land under the mysterious circumstances while Morans come from the seas. Nardians guard the general secret of power that everyone would like to master because it could bring them the unlimited power to rule. They live in a different world, where king Arbatron is hiding them. He is the only one who knows where that place is.

All these groups formed in the long process that all three planets went through. They are the beings of different races, and each of them is already mixed, resulting in a multiethnic universe that has lived in peace without the slightest conflict for three hundred million years. Yes, it's been a long time. The wars of the past have been forgotten. And they weren't just some wars. They almost led to the very demise of life on the three planets. But a breakthrough occurred, and it changed all that hatred into love and mutual respect, into the long-term peace leading to infinity. Yes, it seems impossible, but it may happen. You just need to change your thinking, which was not easy. And that's what this story is going to be about, even though I belong to the generation that is long over. However, that doesn't mean I haven't experienced any conflicts.

The truth is they took place outside this solar system, and I came across them on my journeys through the universe, just like a lot of pilgrims did.

In a nutshell, this is our Asian government which I love very much, and I administrate it with my partner and female administrator Lamesian. Our destined love has gone through difficult trials which have brought us together.

Plant a tree, build a house, and expand the life in it.

Asnians are great builders of life, so great that their kingdom spreads to the different ends of the universe and it shines like a precious gem among the gorgeous glittering jewels. Life they are building enables their society to live in welfare and prosperity, love and mutual respect. During its evolvement, this community has come to such knowledge and effective means that they can work with space so that there is enough for everyone, regardless of their position in the society. They can develop and build life not only in their extraordinary home planetary systems but also in the systems which are parts of a developing civilization. On a suitable planet, which they have chosen for the development of life, they begin to create living conditions that meet the formula for sustaining long-term life there. They have advanced technology in the field of genetics and construction of homelands and thanks to them they can survive an exceptionally long cycle. When they discover a planet with a potential for the development of life and this planet matches their pattern, they use the technology of twenty-one capsules. These capsules are launched into the atmosphere of this planet and thus starts the process which, like a wave of a magic wand, begins to develop everything into an incredible form in an incredibly short time of twenty-one days. Everything begins to bloom and spill. Wonderful clusters of peace-creating and sparkling oceans will emerge, surrounding the beautiful, green, blooming islands. A harmony of magnificent nature full of diverse trees and plants develops and the place flourishes in such splendor that it could be called a paradise. Furthermore, one of the most important processes is the intervention in the magnetosphere, which constructs an effective shield protecting the planet from external adverse influences. Finally, they design, if necessary, an artificial moon to keep the planet in balance. This creates a grouping of planetary nature that is adapted to the planet itself. It is crucial to adapt everything to the very composition and nature of the planet so that it is consistent with the whole cycle, and it lasts. Therefore, things must be prepared, calculated, and studied very precisely to avoid any possible catastrophe. This is the purpose of the expeditions, which are planned so thoroughly that it takes several years to send trained travelers, pilgrims, and their protectors, devoted to their mission since their birth. Yes, these are expeditions that develop life on the alien planets, where they consider it their mission, chosen by an unknown fate. When everything has been done and is ready, the first live entities arrive and test the life on these planets ruled by the travelers. When this process of living and survival on the planet is a success, full colonization and building the society belonging to their creator may begin.

Arkols

Now it is the right time to tell you about our building part. I am going to explain our basic technologies and mention a few points about us and the place where I come from. You can also get the first information necessary to understand us better. Our home planet is Akretium, the main planet of the kingdom of Asnium. (This is something like your capital, because our kingdom comes from three planets that are inhabited by the different species.) It is a beautifully constructed system of magically glowing tears floating in the sky, reaching the great heights. There are several of them and they are home of up to several million creatures. They are diverse, multifunctional, and multi-purpose centres where Asnians find everything they need for their life. Moreover, they do not disrupt the ecosystem of any planet.

Our building technologies are not conventional anymore. Using so called gate technology we can build a solid construction in a snap of fingers and different residential groups and units can move in immediately. These units are divided into various groups, such as planetary and extraplanetary residential units. In addition, there are so-called subgroups that manufacture and supply these complexes. The basic elements are planetary residential central complexes called arkols. Arkols are also specific for their multidimensional living environment inside the complex. We have already figured out how to work with dimensions so that we can make little space larger and thus use this complex as efficiently as possible. In other words, we create interdimensions in the arkol. This enlarged space, scrolled into another dimension, is called akvatium. What does it look like? You unscroll the gate and the synthetic entry to the space opens. Once the gate is opened, the space from the outside looks as if you were looking inside through a magnifying glass. The only difference is that from outside everything seems to be reduced into tiny forms. When you cross the gate shining in the light blue color, you get into another dimension and inside everything is already normal. This is how little space becomes larger. It is a little spell made by an akvatium or multidimension which is intricately connected to the outside world. The whole arkol can be used very effectively because it can accommodate a lot of other complexes. You can put into each the whole city with buildings and houses as well as with artificial nature and many inhabitants. Everyone owns a house with a garden and the city also has other centres, such as entertainment zones and so on. In the residential dimensions in the arkols Asnians will find everything they need to enjoy life and fulfill their needs. I shall remind you that we are quite modest, as we are autotrophic living beings and all we truly need for life is sunlight and water. Actually, these arkols are cities, just hidden in these beautiful shining floating tears of mostly blue color. The color might differ because it depends on the position in the society and the size of the space.

The construction of the arkol lasts three days and it has three stages. Firstly, the builders choose the location very carefully. They study it thoroughly so that they do not spoil anything with their intervention. The location is especially important for the safe operation of the arkol. It cannot be located somewhere where the safety of the population might be endangered. It is also crucial for the functioning of the long-term life cycle. When this process is completed, the construction of the city centre of the arkol begins. It is a relatively interesting process when the builders place a kind of a tubular model in the air in the heart of the selected location. This model, called a toretum, rises to the height and width they have planned and designed. The toretum is made of a noticeably light material called fanx. Inside the toretum, the mantle on the walls is covered with the fluorescent lights. Their name is fequi, they are manufactured stones that glow like yellow and green crystals. They are so-called carriers. They look like rare stones and cover the entire mantle of the inner wall of the toretum. In the middle there is just empty space that will be filled during the construction. On the top of the toretum there are the outlets optically fed to a central satellite in the universe, which is directed at a specific object flying through the space. It can be an asteroid or another object that has been pre-selected and studied so that it can be used for transfer into the toretum to construct the arkol. A quantum device directs the circular beams which decomposes the object into small particles, and these are carried into the prepared toretum. Not only does the device program everything accordingly, but it also starts the construction process. Of course, this construction also begins with the process of stabilization in the air, which is necessary for the operation of the arkol itself.

Secondly, the process of electromagnetic discharges is initiated inside the toretum. Every single stone starts to radiate a discharge of incredible energy. At the same time, the stones begin to interact with each other, and this evokes the energy, in which a solid structure of matter is gradually formed. It begins to merge into the form which the arkol is supposed to have. It's like an image or a photo printed from a computer, except that it's all copied into the real space. Of course, even this method of construction can be dangerous, but only if someone is inside the toretum. It is highly improbable, though. What would one be doing there especially when they are well aware of the fact that any matter there could be decomposed or scattered in a second? So, it is a relatively safe way of building the constructions, which Asnians also use to create a composition of materials extremely specific to the construction of arkols. These are built of incredibly special, but very practical and strong materials adapted to fulfill the purpose in the so-called multidimensionality. After two days and stages inside the toretum, once everything is over, the construction phase of the arkol is completed.

And now it is time for the last stage - the unveiling of a beautiful work. The toretum is assembled and the world can finally see this breathtaking complex that will serve for a very long time, even for ages, depending on the environment in which it has been built. This long duration is also possible thanks to the high-quality material from which the whole complex is made and which we call arx. This material is very firm and yet elastic, and it has a very long life. However, when the life of the arkol itself ends, they cover it again with a toretum and seventeen hours later a reconstructed arkol floats again. It might have even undergone various design changes and modifications if the Asnian administrators of the arkol thought they were necessary. And so everything here turns into an ever-improving splendor, such as Asnium adorned with beautiful jewels that ares floating at enormous heights and contributing to the development of whole of Asnium in the planetary systems.

Admikols

Asnians own another technology which they use to build the objects that are circling around their wonderful planets. It is the second category, the cosmic residential units called admikols. An admikol is a tunnel orbiting the planet and acting as its ring. They are in the orbits around the planets at the same distance as their moons, which are also a part of the ring. Together they form a monolithic ring making the planet even more beautiful. At the same time, they complement the strength of the entire defense mechanism against lurking dangers, and they have also become the seats for living beings. In these rings or cosmic stations created by more rings – admikols – interconnected by very strong elastic tunnels serving as a pass between individual admikols, live a bit different kind of entities called Admans. They are adapted to living conditions in the space, very well trained to fight a potential enemy in any harsh conditions that might pose a threat on various space journeys.

That is why they are also called protectors; they are like universal police or even an army. Admans are smaller in size, but not the shortest, about a medium height of about one hundred and eighty-five centimetres. Moreover, they are heterotrophic beings, which is a paradox, but they feed only on plant foods that they grow in the admikols. Admans have been brought up for space travel since they are little because most of them are already born in the admikols. But this does not mean that they do not visit the home planets of Asnians and do not enjoy their beautiful nature. Many times, it happens that they plan more frequent stays there for a longer period of time, where they are inspired by various spiritual developments of love for each other. And then, rested and filled with the inspiration and understanding of their mission, they return to their homes, admikols.

The admikols are also specific in their multidimensionality, they are bridged by various corridors or tunnels. Inside them there is artificial nature with a large diversity of trees and vegetation created by Asnians themselves, with its own atmosphere that enables full life. A huge amount of water circulates in this environment, flowing like blood through the heart of the admikol. In the middle of the complex there is a giant stone similar to a yellow-burgundy crystal, radiating great and unlimited energy supplying the energy for the operation of the entire admikol. It also acts as a supplier of the additional force needed to support the life cycle in the admikol. This force is gravity. It is this energy, connected to the planetary, gravitational frequency, that is used either to produce energy that drives admikols, or for safe flights among planets, but also admikols.

> The admikols serve as the space stations for communication, navigation, flights to other parts of the universe, but also for the launch of the space crews with the participation of Admans themselves as protectors. They are trained to protect the entire crew from various dangers, whether they are the attacks of unknown hidden enemies or other unpredictable and unknown perils. So, these stations are very closely connected to the life on the planet. Therefore, many Admans, who are born in the admikol, also attend the school centres in the kingdom of Asnium to learn something about the life on the planets. But in

the end, their mission ends in the admikol, from where they get to the different crews, they take a lot of trips and experience adventures outside and inside it. Living conditions in the admikol are not so different from planetary ones. Everything is adapted for the life in them, for a very long-life cycle. So Admans live to be thousand years old, which is not little considering that they are heterotrophic living beings. They have even evolved into another species, and they will be the subject of many legends and stories.

Get unlimited resources to access unlimited energy which will provide you with unlimited power that will drive you on your way to find infinite life.

Another very important element of the Asians' life is energy, which they can produce and process very efficiently. So efficiently that its production and supply is sufficient to provide the entire planet with almost unlimited energy. Their energy production technology is excellent, and it is combined with quantum technology. It is very difficult to understand its principle, but not impossible for Asnians. This principle has given them the basis of knowledge that has pushed their progress so far that it could be called the pinnacle of advances in the field of energy production technology. This energy is essential for quality and unlimited life in welfare where nobody knows the words like poverty, famine, crisis and of course war for positions leading to the domination. Such a counterproductive way of thinking has long been forgotten. Here the beings live in peace, infinite love and understanding, mutual respect regardless the differences in opinions. Mutual respect seems to be an unwritten rule fixed in each of them and came from individual anchoring in the subconsciousness. This is the force that has kept Asnians at peace for so long that they no longer recall when the last conflict among them arose. These can only be found in the ancient legends and myths, which Asnians mention in order not to forget their beloved ancestors. They created not only the conditions for the current state, but also the basis of knowledge leading to the endless and unlimited development of technology. And this technology needs a very large amount of energy, but it brings Asnians not only the development they need to survive on their home planets, but also to develop and colonize the infinite universe which they are a part of.

With this thinking, Asnians came to know about the use of energy, they discovered the technology for its production, which moved them further into the question of life about unlimited existence in eternal prosperity for everybody. It is based on the well-known quantum technology. They can manufacture unbelievably valuable stones that are able to produce energy in different ways and they are amazing. These stones are divided into different categories depending on how they are used.

The first category is G stones, called graxes. Graxes are used frequently and are among the first discoveries of advances in the energy production technology. Actually, it is the first generation of quantum stones used in this world. Grax looks like a huge diamond of light blue colour. It processes the sun rays and transforms them into the energy with almost one hundred per cent efficiency which is enough to supply the whole planet. However, graxes are mainly used to supply the arkols themselves. They are part of the arkols on their top, where they are stored in different numbers depending on the size and extent of these arkols. When such a stone breaks up, it is not a disaster, and the damage is not too bad. Other stones can complement each other until another one is produced and replaces the destroyed or damaged one. It is a very efficient and ecological technology of energy production which does no harm to the environment of such a gorgeous planet.

The second category of quantum stones is multipurpose stones. They produce the energy, and they also provide another form of energy essential for an intelligent form of life – the gravitational force. This force can be produced artificially by means of a certain remarkably interesting form – a stone called frax. These yellow and purple fraxes are used especially in the admikols. They are the cores or hearts of the admikols and they even produce water – both drinking and industrial – which is absolutely necessary for the life inside the admikols. This is done on the basis of the combustion of hydrogen, of which there is essentially an unlimited amount in the space. So even in this way, the admikols create living conditions for Admans.

The third category is dravs. They are small but highly effective stones used as the engines in the cosmic means of transport designed for long travels wherever Asnians need to go in order to simplify their space research. These means of transport are also divided into different categories depending on how they are used.

The first such category is draviats, which are used only for planetary transport by air, amazingly fast, partly semi-automated and very safe. So, if Asnians need to get to a very distant place, it works on the basis of programmable matter, and they can control it through the so-called eagle 's eye. These are small contact lenses that look like very small diamonds. They work like small computers, very powerful and mind controlled. (The Asnian clothing is also based on a programmable matter. It is also controlled by the eagle's eye and can be varied on occasion. It can swiftly be changed when necessary.) The draviats are small boxes that fit in the palm of your hand, but with the help of an eagle's eye we turn them into the means of transport we need. The draviats are the most widely used means of transport, which looks like a well-shaped arrow made of a very strong diamond-like material (various colors of your choice). Each draviat has its own flight path. This means that the display shows a virtual path leading to the destination where Asnian needs to get. Transport by draviats is controlled by a central system from the space. This ensures that the routes of the draviats do not collide with each other. The slower flying draviats can be safely overtaken. So sometimes during the day, it looks as if a lot of diamonds are flying here and there at enormous speed in the sky. The drive of the draviats is so quiet that you can only hear very gentle whistling. Their powerful engines are powered by unlimited energy, which is supplied by stones called dravs.

The second category of means of transport is a dravatec. It is intended for interplanetary transports of individuals or transports to the admikols. There are also means of public transport called draviatechs. These are already like your planes, but they have our typical features and properties, depending, naturally, on whether they are dravatecs or draviatechs.

Asnians also have a third category of means of transport, but these are intended only for public and strictly planned transport. As propulsion they don't use just the dravs, but also technology using another type of a stone, which already belongs to another category. These stones are not designed to produce energy but create bridges - a kind of shortcuts - to move among different parts of the universe. This means of transport is called gravtas. Gravtases are long tubes that can very deftly traverse various terrains and bridge those tunnels, i.e. shortcuts to the different parts of the universe, without wasting time. They can reach tremendous speeds, but that's not an important element. Bridging is essential. Of course, gravtases also have aquatias (the multidimensional technology mentioned in the Arkols chapter) as well as fraxes, which provide them not only with the artificial gravity, but also with everything they need to survive while traveling through the space.

Well, this is a brief account on our energy, the stones and means of transport available to Asnians.

Agenkols are the training centres, individual units, or cities for
our young generations. They are the strong pillars of the Asnian
society. They are the future which will develop their world. The
world they have spent years to build so that everybody can live
happily in unlimited prosperity. This whole world also depends on
the future generation, on how well-educated it will be, how it will
govern in an effort to at least maintain its level if not even
improve it, to develop the reserves for even greater welfare,
happiness, love and peace.

The agenkols educate children since they are 5 years old. Children keep staying there until they reach the level showing their focus and vocation they will follow during their life in this world. As soon as they reach the age of five, they automatically take the talent tests. They will categorize them into five groups and will determine in which direction they could proceed on the path to fulfilling their mission. From the age of five, children are separated from their parents, which does not mean that they do not visit each other from time to time. Children will attend a ten-month training in the centre and then there will be a two-month break which has nothing to do with the seasons. It is more about maintaining at least some family ties and about a little fun. It doesn't mean there is no fun in the agenkols, quite the opposite. Their teachers and educators take care of that.

Each school centre has seven grades and each grade lasts five years according to the classification of the department. There are two categories. The cosmic mission means preparing for life in the universe and developing its life. The second category concerns the planetary and interplanetary mission. None of the categories is inferior, as they bring classification to the different groups in the hierarchy of the society. It isn't not about who is more valuable and who is less, because the planetary mission also includes the education and training of children in the school centres. Furthermore, the talent can manifest itself in various spheres. But those who fall into the category of a space mission have a better chance of becoming space travelers, or, if they pass all seven degrees in the agenkols, also the pilgrims, which is the highest rank in the space missions. The pilgrims are in the leadership of the expeditions and are responsible for the lives of the entire crews. But for an Asnian to become a pilgrim, it is not enough to complete seven degrees in the agenkol. They must also take part in a lot of expeditions. Only then they can obtain this rank. However, it doesn't stop here. If they manage to reach the age of ten thousand years, or their immortality is confirmed, they can enter the global government belonging to the Council of Elders or the Council of Sages who have the potential to become the administrators of the government. The administrators come from a handful of the immortal individuals who have achieved the highest level of awareness and both knowledge and spiritual development. Even though there are no limits and borders, this is the highest level of awareness ever documented. Only the pilgrims and administrators are able to achieve it. These are the rules that have been set during the development of the society. It is impossible to become a member of the government without knowledge and experience necessary to take the responsibility for the life of all Asnians and also for themselves and their acts.

Let's get back to the agenkols. They are the same everywhere and they can educate up to eleven million children. They employ more than four million teachers, professors and educators whose job is to help children to obtain knowledge and develop their spirituality in the seven grades since it is what they need to find their place in life and fulfill their mission. Some individuals drop out after the third grade because they have decided to set on the planetary or interplanetary mission. However, if one day they discover that their mission might be elsewhere, they can aways come back and finish school. This happens very rarely, but quite a lot of the pilgrims have later been able to pass the talent tests leading to the cosmic knowledge. Therefore, the actual purpose of the first three grades is to provide both categories with similar cognition leading that will help them to get knowledge and find their life path.

The next four grades are higher. The individuals acquire different qualifications for different kinds of mission. Of course, these grades are focused also on the planetary mission if Asnians would like to get qualifications for a higher mission. Everyone has a chance to get to the forefront of the social hierarchy, no matter where they come from. But in the kingdom of Asnium, despite the existence of a certain social hierarchy, no differences are made. Beings treat each other with respect, regardless of their position and mission in the society. Here we all love each other, and we are happy together as one family, whether planetary or interplanetary. We do not force anyone into anything here, nor do we interfere in the societies that want to be independent of us. Therefore, the government treats other independent civilizations with respect, tries not to interfere and possibly learn from them. Every civilization brings something interesting and instructive. We do not classify them at all as inferior in the hierarchy of the cosmic society of diverse civilizations.

It is crucial that the civilizations treat each other with respect, friendliness, and love. That is why we are trying to communicate with you very carefully. You are an independent civilization with its own hierarchy, which we Asnians respect, and you are a benefit to us, we have learnt a lot from you. And we hope that when you get to know our civilization, when I tell you about many interesting stories from our history, we will be friends. And you too will find a way to be an even more advanced civilization that will honor every life in the universe. But in order to achieve such a state, you have to break out of your comfort zone, you have to defeat your main enemy. And that enemy is you.

Learning about the universe

The universe is a beauty and yet a mystery and a call for great knowledge. We have been trying to find out more about our origin for a long time and we've come quite far. However, it's hard to explain it to you. I can understand that you are very curious about what we've found out. I've already told you about how we use quantum physics, but that's just a drop in the ocean. Don't worry, though. I am going to tell you the legend of our origin. We also have a lot of stories and legends about our heroes who sacrificed their lives for our existence and about the wars of domination. Yes, even we have been formed by various wars. The wars we had fought for ages before we found our peace. There are a lot of stories about those ages too, the stories I will tell you when the time is right.

Well, where to start, so you can understand our distant existence? We are extremely far from you, up to several billion light years. But I will not burden you with our location in the space. I will begin with knowledge because the universe created us and everything around us. The big bang is the beginning of everything. Giant dark matter looking like an infinite cluster of the dark clouds in one huge pile which creates a large circle, the largest that may ever be formed in our visible universe. This circle is very wild, full of the lightnings as if it was a violent storm. Dark matter needs dark energy for its existence. Dark energy needs the energy of light that it keeps absorbing until it consumes it all. Once all the light, matter and dust and its surroundings run out, dark energy runs out too. Dark matter begins to collapse into itself, huge friction comes, and small particles of matter that have fallen into infinite singularities awaken again, and a big bang is formed. And not only one, but they are also more, surrounding this circle. All the matter of dust and huge light triggers an unimaginable chain reaction and dark energy is awakened to life. It begins to expand until all the light again surrounds the entire circle and a stable hyper galaxy is formed, a galaxy of all galaxies. Everything revolves and expands around the circle, and it has its hierarchy. The galaxy has a black hole in the middle and in the centre of the hyper galaxy there is vast dark matter in the shape of a circle full of clouds, dust, lightnings and whirls that create unbelievably strong gravitation. There are many such hyper galaxies, and they are active, but they are unimaginably far away. It is impossible to reach them. Even our technology hasn't gone far enough to explore them. But we've already seen at least a very small piece. All we know is that the universe is a vast and endless labyrinth.

And this is where our story begins. Or shall I call it a fairy tale or perhaps a legend? I am going to share a story written by our king Arbatron himself. These are his words and I hope you will like them. Have fun, my dear people.

The Legend of the Stones of Life

Soul – is like a small feather that has disengaged itself from a bird which is flying into the unknown. This feather is just soaring in the infinite space, unable to do anything but let the wind carry it wherever the fate will take it. Soul has fallen into its singularity where it lives in the never-ending dreamland. When there are more of them together, they will find the way to their common dream that will come true eventually. They will create their common world where they will be trying to lead full but not eternal life. They will get a physical body and wake up from their singularity or dream. When they finally leave their body, they will fall into the singularity and their dreamland again. It goes around like this in circles until they find the way leading to eternal life. And this is their mission.

There are small indivisible particles, the tiniest of all, indestructible and immortal. They don't have physical bodies, just consciousness which is only like an observer without a chance to control anything and is simply watching what is going on. But in the end, they figured out how to influence what was happening around them. They came with the big bang and were a part of something unknown, something they couldn't even imagine in their mind or fantasy. They have been wandering through the universe since its inception. It might even be said that they were involved in creation of what we can see now.

These particles can save so much information that you might store an infinite number of lives in them. They are spreading in the space, a lot of particles together. Together they are stronger, and they can do the impossible. The information is flying through the space, looking for the way how to incarnate into something material, something that could be controlled and then to make the space of their own and lead full life in this unknown world. When they finally succeeded, they came across the setbacks they had not anticipated. They had to deal with them before they created their common tangible world where they could develop their material life. They managed to settle down and stabilize their life. However, it turns out they have been failing to maintain this material life in the long term. Their creations, though still improving, are imperfect.

Another drawback is the differences in opinions on where to go next. There are two groups of these particles with different beliefs, named the particles of light and the particles of darkness. Due to this division, there has been a struggle for space and the direction of their material life, as well as for existence in the universe. Therefore, different worlds are created, and different groups are looking for the most optimal composition that could survive even the most unfavorable conditions. They can face various enemies who have been trying to destroy their beautiful material world for ages. However, both groups have one disadvantage: When they finally attain the material existence, their life starts from the beginning. They don't remember their origin; they are in the dissimilar and very complex structure of perception of their own consciousness. In this moment, the universe becomes their real home, where they are starting from the very beginning, looking for the way how to stay alive as long as possible, even forever. This is the main aim of souls: to create their own material world, survive in it and try to develop it.

And here comes the question: Where do the souls that can remember their origin only in the spiritual form come from? This is what the souls are attempting to solve in the material state: How to find the way to themselves, to survive in the material world and develop the universe into absolute splendor that will provide them with all they need to stay alive. The answer is: to overcome the obstacles and pass the trials. However, the universe surprised them here. They learnt that the universe was their ruler and it divided them into two groups. This was when they understood that they were just at the beginning when it came to knowledge. The thing is, that there is a small group of souls that have all this knowledge of the universe stored in their memory. It is hidden in the material cluster where their memories have been temporarily eliminated by the system in some unknown spacetime.

Universe – is a fairy tale whose beginning and ending remain unknown to all living beings in the material world. It is an endless labyrinth with endless time spaces, and it seems that, for some reason, its purpose is to punish those disobedient particles which need to learn something if they would like to escape from this labyrinth. And this is awfully hard for them as they remember nothing in the material world. It resulted in the infinite mechanism kept alive by the cycle of origin and extinction, the cycle of life and death and movement of everything inside. It gives the impression of a perfect machine that controls everything and is nourished by an infinite number of time spaces. These time spaces are its crucial part because they produce vast and infinite energy which keeps this mechanism alive. All time spaces interact with each other just as everything inside them interacts with everything else and with itself. At first glance it looks as if it was all perfect. However, some very brave living beings found certain cracks and thus discovered the least probable parts of the mechanism. They were living forms, particles in the material world that had got to the certain level of consciousness, they had remembered and found their true self. They immediately started to have doubts and wanted to change the system but were stopped by a very tough barrier that the mechanism had placed to block their way. This mechanism has an extremely powerful defense system whose purpose is to protect it from any possible destruction and prevent from creating something better and nicer or just something different from this cold and cruel world. Therefore, its mission was to cast a curse upon these living particles and make them stay in an even deeper cycle of life and death, so they were unable to recall anything, and they served the system of endless interacting cycles.

No living form can recollect how this mechanism came into being. And another enormously powerful weapon enters the game - time. More and more times are running, and the cursed living forms are engaged in nonsense such as hatred, envy, greed and desire for unlimited power over something they can no longer even name. They have no idea what they are part of. There have been so many cycles of so many living forms that it can't even be counted. There is an infinite number of legends, and their beginning is so distant that no one can remember it. But there is one small crack. Everything has its memory after all, even though it is blurred and hidden in the subconsciousness of the mechanism of consciousness. And that consciousness has created a defense system that is transmitted through all those infinite time spaces nicely scattered throughout that mechanism.

The mechanism encounters one noticeably big obstacle: Sometimes creatures with strong souls - we can call them prophets – appear and they remember. The mechanism attempts to destroy them by fate immediately and thus send their souls to the beginning of their existence in the material world. But destiny is a double-edged sword, because even the mechanism that creates destiny has its own destiny, that it is rebelling against. Therefore, there will be living forms with extraordinarily strong mental will, which may eventually find that small crack in the mechanism and also a way how to become immortal in their material bodies. And they may fight against the cycle of life and death. The truth is that it is a ridiculously hard and complicated path. A living form needs a huge amount of time to develop well enough to jog its memory and learn a bit about how the system works. Firstly, it must somehow function in this mechanism, go hand in hand with it and accept its rules. It is not necessary to follow these rules all the time, just enough to trick the system. However, the mechanism has improved itself so much that it is almost impossible to find the way how to stop it. But the living forms never give up, their courage and desire to find something better keeps pushing them forward and they are fighting fiercely in this fight with windmills. Finally, they realized that in the universe, anything is possible. They found the most powerful weapon – fantasy and power of their souls that help them create whatever they like.

Later they came across another obstacle. They found out that so many living forms had already arisen before them that had tried to change the mechanism, that they had already been forgotten, and it was the same strong souls who had left a very significant trace to help them jog their memory again. But who were the first and strong ones who had found the courage to fight this imperfect mechanism? No one can remember that anymore, but they have left such a clear trace behind them that it cannot be erased from the subconsciousness of the souls and this mechanism. There have been so many fights here that only visionaries can discover the trace. After countless life forms, the decisive life one emerged. With admirable will of its soul, it began to create a very strong body structure, which is still alive and bravely resists the strong defense system of the mechanism. These structures have found such strong energy that even the mechanism cannot cope with them now, because they are using its own power. It is the power of light and darkness, which is also a part of the mechanism, it is its weapon. But the creatures have learnt that the mechanism can only be controlled and defeated by its own weapons which can be mastered by the will of very old and strong souls, who have created such strong and resilient bodies that they have become very capable opponents of this mechanism. They call them the first souls, who came with the big bang from the multiple time spaces. And therefore, in this decisive struggle, two kingdoms with extraordinary beings were created. These beings are immortal kings who hate and try to control each other, so their secret is hidden rather behind the hatred that controls them. And this is where the most important tale about the kingdoms of the immortal kings and their remarkably close servants, who serve as an army of immortal warriors, begins. It was the form of power that entered this dispute over infinite space when certain forms of life had already managed to figure out how to become immortal. It began with two kings from very, very, very ancient times, when life in the universe was just beginning to be aware of itself and look for a way to survive all those clashes and conflicts in one of the infinite numbers of time spaces. The cycle of extinction and creation was much wilder again. But the living beings acquired the ability to adapt to the different conditions. They must have had great strength, extraordinarily strong will to live, even so strong that it finally defeated all the side effects which were trying to destroy them. That's what life is all about. You just have to defeat all the side effects around you and inside you and try to break your way to your own being. And what do we consider animate or inanimate? The universe is full of both, so it is impossible to specify what is and what is not animate. But these two kings managed to defeat the side effects that were trying to destroy them. Thus begins the Legend of the Stones of Life, written by Arbatron himself.

The big bang happened and suddenly everything lit up again.

2

Oh, I can see you, my dear souls, I can see you in that flash of light which is carrying you away from me. Away to the darkness where the light expands and you, my dear souls, are leaving me. My heart is breaking, and I am hurting when I see this happening. But don't you worry, my dear souls, the time will come, and you will break the curse that has been cast on you and the good old times and the eternity which has been both our gift and curse and which we have lost will return. Just try not to forget, you must remember your past moments, who you used to be, what you used to be, where you used to be. Don't be afraid of those dark forces, they are not omnipotent and invincible, just be careful with their guards. They will be very convincing; they will attempt to control you and persuade you about your powerlessness and ignorance. And when the truth about your eternity, excellence and indestructibility will be close, they will do their best to hide your memory in material bodies. They will assign the tasks to you in their dark world which now believes that it has gained the control over the power of light. But it is just their pride and desire for power which will eventually become their end. Their own greed and desire to keep the eternity for themselves alone will turn them into soulless puppets that have no idea what love is. And love will become the key element which will destroy the dark forces and they will be forgotten by history; they will cease to exist in the eternity of love and understanding.

I love you, my dear souls. Please keep in your mind that I, Arbatron, am the king of love and mercy. One day you will recognize me and when at least one soul will do so, everything will change. The forces of darkness will suffer the greatest defeat they have never even dreamt of in their worst nightmares, they will be gone, together with their rule over the entire world of endless possibilities. This message was delivered to all the souls by the big bang while they were wandering together with the light. These little souls, these tiny invisible and indestructible particles are not aware of anything yet. They are still sleeping in the thickset of light that is surrounding them and forming into beauty. The universe itself is not quite sure what their story will be, what to prepare in cooperation with the dark forces.

The souls are wandering like disengaged feathers of birds, and they don't know yet whether they already exist. They keep strolling and have no idea what fate, what awakening into new life that no one knows what it will be like, is awaiting them. The light and fires of all the worlds are spreading in the infinite and dark space. Darkness is building up its kingdom and its consciousness that will rule over those dear souls. They will feed on its energy which will bring them endless possibilities of world creation in the infinite beginnings and endings. The universe is starting to cool down, the first worlds made by wonderful nebulas of dust and shining stars are emerging. The dark forces are celebrating because they can turn their own craving into material bodies and rule just as their immaterial bodies are dreaming about it. The nice little soul particles have started dreaming as well although their world is just beginning to form and they don't know where they are, what this means and what is around them. However, the dark forces have noticed and become aware of their power therefore they are already influencing their new dreamland with their own projections. They have instilled in them a small seed of an idea, harmless to souls - the idea of desire. The particles don't know what it is yet, but it is already spreading like cancer in their new dreamland. Their memory has been pushed back. They don't remember the lovely world that has been here before their current material one, which is now forming and has pulled them into the curse of life and death, inception and extinction. They have begun to perceive the world around, in which they have just woken up. They can't understand what their eyes are looking at. But it is developing. Their dreamland is still somewhere between the material and immaterial world. They are perceiving the material world. It has become their desire which shall create the world. The world which the dark forces would be unable to build because their big weakness is the absence of the creative mind – fantasy, which is excellently developed in the souls of light.

At present, the dark forces are ruling over the souls of light. They are dominating their developing dreamland too. However, nothing has been created there yet, so the dark forces are trying to influence the souls of light and make them use their gift of world creating to build the world that will serve the purposes of the dark forces. The souls of life long for this beautiful world and they have begun to produce the dream projections, something like paintings on dream canvas. The souls of darkness like it but the lord of darkness is becoming impatient as this is still not enough for him. The souls of light – and all other ones - have just one goal: material bodies that don't exist yet. And this is a collective desire that the dark forces put inside the souls of light in a form of a thought. The souls of light are working on the proposals on what the bodies and the world where they will all live in, shall look like. As the time passes, the lord of darkness is satisfied with the work of the souls of light. Just one more step and everything will be set into motion. The souls are influencing the developing material world which is at the stage of offering other possibilities of self-creation. With their dreamworld, the souls are influencing the objects, but these are hardly forming in the shape the souls want them to. The dark forces can't understand what is going wrong. The lord of darkness is frustrated. He craves his material body so much that he is unaware of all the laws present in the forces of light and the fact that it is not unchallenging to control them. Furthermore, if you try to control them, it might easily turn against you. The lord of darkness has just realized one thing – it is the unity of the souls of light that can prove impossible, and they know it. He feels that it may be a huge risk. When the souls are united, they are invincible and collectively they are able to control the power of light and the matter that is being developed in this new world of endless possibilities. The lord of darkness has decided to take the risk but he will scatter the dark forces among those souls of light so they can supervise the whole process of creation and he will be engaged in this too. We can see the material world emerging, now controlled also by another beautiful power. Everything is spinning, all matter is interacting with itself in this labyrinth of life and death, inception and extinction.

Arbatron can see this, but he is not able to intervene, because it is the immaterial past that he is watching, powerless. "Oh, my dear souls, don't worry, I will find the way out of this. I am sure some souls will finally remember and overturn everything. The lord of darkness is not so perfect, and he will make a mistake once. It's simple, when someone wants to control this power, they must be aware of the fact that they might be controlled by the world of imperfection and mistakes."

Arbatron knows there is just one more strength left. Hope. All souls are united, driven by the common desire to build a paradise which will bring them something wonderful. They are collectively influencing individual objects, just like when you push the first domino and the next domino in line will be knocked over and then the next... But not to destroy everything, quite the opposite. To create the world most suitable for them. When you are making up a puzzle, you simply must know the rules. Only the souls of light are familiar with these rules because it is their power. The lord of darkness is taking the risk. He must open a small part of the memory of the souls of light and let them enter their dreamland so they can start to make up the world from the matter. The souls, like a swarm of bees, are influencing every piece of the puzzle, and the pieces are falling into their place. But also, the dreamland is being formed into an even more incredible beauty, which surpasses the newly formed world of matter. The individual parts kept bumping into each other and formed the dreamland of the dark king, who, however, kept the souls of light under control. It took a long time for the world of matter to take shape. The dark king was angry. He longed for the material world so much that he began to be consumed by impatience. He constantly influenced the unsuspecting souls of light with his anger, he kept bombarding them with one desire - the motivation that the world of matter would be beautiful, would be their paradise, where they could experience knowledge, they had not even thought of in their dreamland.

After such a lot of failures, the material world finally formed into its entire beauty and created the conditions for full life. The dark king could not believe it. He was extremely happy and so were the dark souls and forces. The souls of light were excited too, although they had no idea how they were going to be deceived in this material world. The souls don't know what hatred, envy, desire to fight and control is. All they do know is love, mutual respect and life full of games – something that ruling dark forces have never heard of. Therefore, the laws of darkness remain for the world of darkness, and the laws of light for the world of light. As one force seeks to control the other, it must realize that the laws of the other world will use its weapons against it. And the dark forces — since a new material world had just been created to be common to both the light world and the dark world — did not anticipate that even laws could be easily interconnected, they did not have to suit either side.

Well, and finally, one more surprise awaited the forces of darkness: In this new world, new laws apply only to the material world. And when the dark forces enter the material world, they will not remember anything, because it is another dimension of life that will control you before you get the chance to control it.

And so, the unsuspecting souls of darkness and light set about creating a new stage of life.

3.

Among a lot of stars and astronomical objects a new planet was born. It was beautiful and blue, it circled around the star like a diamond and this star gave this marvelous world incredible power. All the souls, either dark or light, admired this world eager to take another step in its development, this unbelievable dream that had just become real and tangible. The dreamland used to be wonderful too, but it was lacking anything that could be perceived by the sense of touch. It offered endless possibilities without any laws but the material world, which the lord of darkness found hard to believe they had managed to create, could do the same. There was just one small step to take, the last and hardest of all the steps, as the lord said to the souls. They knew that this step would necessarily bring about a clash. It would be the clash of life that would complete this gorgeous masterpiece once and for all.

50

Therefore, all dark and light souls together gained control over several objects and directed them to this amazing planet waiting to be colonized by the entities that would live here in this spectacular world. Like a swarm of bees, they settled down on the giant objects, on the stones of life where all the souls had just begun to get ready to fly into this lovely blue gem and prepare everything, they needed to cook the essence of life in the alluring world of immaterial souls they had been dreaming of. The souls smaller than that smallest particle, the souls hiding in the stars, where they are living their dream. Now they proved impossible, they gained control over the objects which they directed like some means of transport to this wonderful material world they are going to colonize to be able to taste a delicious cake of life, piece by piece and thus enter another stage of life – a fight between darkness and light. The peculiar thing is that even darkness might be beautiful and there can be something good and evil hiding behind the desire. And here we will see whether the dark forces are right or if the forces of light will enforce their truth about beauty and love. That is something they will surely want to do in this world. However, they will have to face a great obstacle, the forces of darkness, which have just connected with the power of light, and we can just guess who will win this battle. The forces of darkness are at an advantage, because after a certain event they have ostensibly managed to gain control of the forces of light. The stones of life are flying into the atmosphere of the dazzling world. They are falling down to the ground and their fall launches a new era of life in the new unknown world, the era of a labyrinth of all labyrinths of life and death, inception and extinction, in which the dominant power will be manifested.

The game of life has just begun.

4.

The stones of life began bombarding this awesome world which is screaming: "Ouch, what the hell is going on? Everything has already been in balance and now it is changing!" Huge explosions of fire are warming up the astonishing world, the seas are boiling, the fires are pouring down and the whole world is upside down. But after some time, everything starts to calm down, just time, awfully long time begins ticking, having launched the cooking of the essence of life. The souls are working together, supporting each other because all they are just creating is based on their common effort. The whole system of life is made up of the uniform and cooperating particles of souls operating in a certain unspoken hierarchy, where one soul, the one with the highest consciousness, will eventually become the consciousness of the entire system, which they are trying to create in the whirl of dust, sand and water. These basic building blocks are being boiled together, first creating small simple systems which are then combined into more

52

complex ones that are working together with water and rocks. They are stirring it all until they manage to create something. It takes ages to form it, it's still quite imperfect, so far without any features, it's a mass like gelatine. Thus, organic and automated matter is created, and it is waiting for the souls to control it. They finally succeed in creating at least a foundation, a very flawed brain. The first signs of consciousness begin to appear inside it, the consciousness which is just about to enjoy something new at least for a while, something it does not yet know.

Something unbelievable happened. The souls of darkness and light together created something appealing and mysterious that they all like. The new forms of life came into existence, although they are still rather primitive and therefore it is hard to say whether they could be called the form of life which perceives something. But they can feel the environment of the sea, something that no single soul felt before. They can feel something cold blowing and making them chilly. It is just an imperfect larva without limbs, only one immature torso but able to master a movement in this world. Suddenly in that sea you can see countless larvae being carried away by the waves and all souls are enjoying it. But in the end, after not even such a long time, they lose these sketchy bodies again, and return to the immaterial consciousness. But there are already organic and automated substances on the planet, which, through trial and error, are trying to create something that could already look like a full-fledged life form.

A lot of water passes under the bridge and the larvae are beginning to change into something more complex. The souls are working together very tenaciously to create something that would already give shape to this quintessential creature, who could fully enjoy that splendid unknown material world offering many opportunities for a full life. From the vortex of cells and proteins, rocks, dust and water, something more complex is beginning to form. Their strong and collective consciousness led by the dark forces, is just finding out what is necessary for a full-fledged creature to emerge. This creature already has the first limbs and entrails needed to control this whole machine and function in this world. The consciousness manages to perceive this world even more perfectly, being even more fascinated it can move at the bottom of the sea. However, other creatures also began to form according to the imagination of souls working together to create the diversity of life and according to their ideas of how they could function in the material world. They found out from the cells themselves that they were missing something. It is the energy that the organism needs and so from the very beginning, primitive organisms begin to consume each other. The paradox is that this is what gave birth to a creature connected by large clusters of the cells eating each other. They are still working very tenaciously and spewing out the ideas on how to create the most perfect creature in which they could exist as fully as possible in this world. They have even figured out how to simplify reproduction so that they do not have to spend so much energy on creating the life forms - they have divided the creatures into males and females. Many small seahorses have emerged, also small snails and they are starting to enjoy their life, but they are not able to keep it for long. They are leaving the world; they are constantly collapsing, and the souls still do not comprehend it. However, they solved it in no time, and the lord of darkness understood it very quickly. The creature is missing something especially important. Energy. The souls managed a very clever move, they used proteins to create a living structure and they fed on it and thus replenished their energy.

Once they solved this tricky issue, the various creatures began to develop beautifully, because they were now able to draw the energy for a longer life in this world. A new structure emerged, it swam up to the water surface and was carried away by the waves. Then another structure came into existence, and it was autotrophic living organisms that slowly evolved into even more complex structures. They drew the energy from the light and water and thus more and more complex and perfect creatures were emerging because the living conditions were finally more than convenient.

This was the era when the law of dark souls was passed: the souls support each other and the soul which is the lucky one and becomes superior with higher consciousness lives on the expense of the inferior souls that must support the highest one. This had already been decided in the dreamland, which had been the mirror of the current one. Unfortunately, the souls of light were unaware of this injustice and were happy to help each other by creating the autotrophic living organisms that didn't need this law to survive in the long term. The souls of darkness didn't participate in this, and they were mostly just superior souls of consciousness so they could enjoy the material world and the life in it. Although they didn't remember their origin when they entered their new bodies, or what they were looking for, as they hadn't solved the mystery of how to remember. It was the lord of darkness who wanted to figure out how to make this program in the brain of the creatures. The souls of light served him very diligently and made more and more fitting bodies for him. A diverse world was beginning to emerge, and the souls of light were excited. It was the mysterious world that the dark lord had no idea about. But he could program at least one thing in the creatures: Although he did not know how, he wanted to show the souls of light who would ultimately be the master of the material world. But with that, he made a rod for his own back, and he didn't even realize it yet. The creatures controlled by the consciousness of darkness made it easier for themselves, they began to feed on those peaceful creatures and recharged their energy. They started to eat the peaceful entities, who understood nothing. This marked the beginning of the fight for control of this world and the game of "survival of the fittest" began. Everyone ate up everyone else, from the tiniest and most primitive creature to the biggest one.

At the sea level, the autotrophic living beings began to develop slowly. They arose as hope for a turn of events in this magnificent world.

5.

The creatures of this world were finally divided into the peaceful ones, living just on light and water and the creatures' called predators, eating up other weaker creatures. The predators evolved over time, whether intellectually or through the perfection of their bodies. They were more deceitful, wiser, stronger and their most powerful weapon was very well-developed teeth, but other parts of their bodies also gained in quality. Moreover, they learnt that their source of food is limited, so they let the weaker creatures reproduce and develop and thus gave them a slight chance for further development. The evolution of the predators went hand in hand with the evolution of the peaceful creatures on the water surface. That started an incredible evolution. The predators evolved even more, and somewhere in that dream they developed their subconsciousness that helped them to realize at least a little of the origin of their souls. The only thing that held the world of the creatures together, so that the souls had certain motivation and believed coming back there was worthy, was the faith that this world was exquisite, and they felt excellent there. Their life here had other purpose than just be a soul without a body. And this motivated both sides to return to this manufactured paradise. Somewhere in that dream subconsciousness was born and helped the souls to be aware of their origin a little.

However, the lord of darkness was dissatisfied. In the end, he always had to leave this world because they hadn't been able to make the bodies perfect enough to endure forever. He also struggled with another variable, and that was the wear and tear of the bodies, which eventually became old. Thus, death arose and sent the souls back to the immaterial world. They had to find the right host again in which they could start living all over. This is just what the material world is like. It isn't flawless, but everything can be worked on to even greater perfection. Therefore, the creatures continued to evolve further and further into even more remarkable creations, until at last the most perfect beings that the souls of darkness and the souls of light managed to create together, appeared. The souls of darkness finally discovered the secret world of the souls of light, and this infuriated the lord of darkness. But he let it be since he had realized another advantage of this division: They could learn a lot from the souls of light, because their creations became more and more ideal and diverse. The souls of darkness took the advantage of this. They produced more ideal predators to be able to attack the world of the souls of light. But as time flew by, even the souls of light began to feel there was something wrong, that they were being watched and endangered, but they couldn't still explain what exactly it meant. They developed extraordinarily strong abilities - premonition, for example - but they did not know that they were controlled by the dark forces, because they did not know what the dark forces were. But eventually one soul of light began to wonder why in the material world everything happened the way it did. This soul knew it must not reveal that it knew anything or what it knew, but over time it found out that something was controlling them. And it kept returning to the material world and gaining experience, trying to figure out what was going on. From now on, it, too, tried to motivate other souls inconspicuously to create more and more perfect beings on the surface of the sea, so that they could possibly defend themselves against the danger. However, this played into the lord's of the darkness hands because he liked the newer ideal bodies enjoying the fabulous moments in the material world of fear more and more. A cat-and-mouse game started. The more aware soul got at the root of the problem and figured out who was behind that all because also the immaterial dreamland developed into beauty, but it was not possible to experience there the same things as in the material world. And they began to call this world a paradise.

Sooner or later, quite perfect creatures were created in the material world. The dark lord decided to enter an immensely powerful entity, and in his subconsciousness, he had stored the idea that he would someday figure out how to become immortal. However, he knew that he had to find a very strong host capable not only of withstanding the harsh conditions, but also of controlling other creatures. Thus, his dream might come true in the end, and he might be able to establish an ultimate kingdom, in which he would be a king and he would rule this paradise forever. But he did not know that he was being watched by the conscious soul of light. When he entered the material world, this soul immediately found others whom it trusted and told them what it had revealed. They found it hard to believe, but it was clear that they had to do something. This was when a small group of souls was formed and decided to fight against these dark forces.

This was what they finally named them. The dark forces. To stay safe and not to lose the upper hand, they didn't spread the facts any further, they let the other souls unaware of the truth. They called themselves the prophets. They stored this into their subconsciousness in which they would try to reveal their origin while living in the material world and face their enemy. They don't understand him yet and they have no idea what they are up against, but it is the beginning of the conviction that the lord of darkness is not invincible, he just doesn't know about it yet. And so over time, these prophets also created more convenient hosts for themselves to be able to enter this world and defeat the lord of darkness.

6

Once upon a time, somewhere in the dark depths, after a long, long time, a very cruel dark predator emerged. He was later named Alegon. He was also an autotrophic living being, but unlike others he took his energy from the darkness. He was an incredibly sad lord because he was one of his kind. First, he conquered the dark army of Feriases, who protected his dark world. Feriases had huge heads, black skin and four tusks in their mouths, adorned with razor-sharp teeth. Their biggest disadvantage was that they hated the light. They were heterotrophic organisms, which fed on other creatures. However, even this race was unable to put the autotrophic beings on the surface in peril. Therefore, the evolution of the desire of the dark souls created another species, an overly aggressive kind of species, which was a great threat to the unsuspecting celestial beings, as the predators began to call them. This species developed gradually. It was a shark species, warriors completely devoted to Alegon. They managed to survive in the dark depths of the ocean but also near the surface which made them a strong candidate. However, there was another predator that could compete with the shark one and it was a crocodile species, but it had noticeably big shortcomings. They were all loners, not unanimous in their opinions and they often got into conflicts with each other. The shark species was an amazingly effective weapon of Alegon, the lord of the dark depths. This lord had a huge desire to get to the heavens, but he had to find a way how to do that because he was a dark being. And it was the shark species that could help him accomplish this goal.

The sharks eventually evolved to gain limbs, legs, and arms; they became very intelligent and had the ability to kill effectively. Their close species, sharks, exceptionally large sharks, served them well as a means of transport, so they were actually both a very efficacious weapon and means of transport. After a certain time and never-ending struggles came the moment of a lord of this kind. His name was Eld Ion, and he was an extremely cruel and deceitful warrior. He had to slaughter many living things to become the lord of this savage species. He often made his way to the surface itself and watched his first prey among celestial creatures who did not know yet what killing and the struggle for survival were.

They were celestial and very pure creatures supposed to be ruled by intelligent, peaceful, and loving Ardax. At the beginning, the celestial creatures used only one name, which was rather a nickname. Sometimes their names meant something, sometimes they didn't, and they were just the figments of their imagination. They knew nothing about violence, anger and hatred, envy and pride or fury. Eliah, Ardax's brother and his beloved Etes were enjoying having their first child. She was still a little girl who was just smiling fondly at her parents. They were right below the surface because just like all celestial creatures they lived high in the underwater mountains, they were standing at the very top of the mountain to admire the dazzling play of the rays coming from the star they couldn't see. They didn't know what the star or night sky were, let alone what that world around them was like. Eliah was just holding his little princess Ilemis in his arms and Etes was smiling happily when suddenly an unexpected horror came like a bolt from the blue. A shark with a large open mouth and Eld Ion sitting on its back. The shark bit off Etes's head right in front of the eyes of unsuspecting Eliah, who did not know what to do. Eld's massive spear went straight through Etes's body. However, when he aimed at Eliah, he did not hesitate for a second and immediately took to flight with little Ilemis still in his arms. The vicious shark with sharp teeth was trying to catch Eliah, but he was escaping very deftly and intelligently. Eld was trying to stab him, and they got between two hills. On one of them there was the entrance to the mountain, which was already full of celestial beings having fun and enjoying their time. Eliah just shouted telepathically Help! The unwary celestial creatures grabbed everything at hand and attacked the ferocious shark creatures. Eld and his shark recovered very quickly and began to escape, satisfied even with that little loot he had caught. He took a bite of something unknown, and he liked it. He liked it even so much that he longed for it. He let other shark creatures to try it too and thus he wanted to motivate his subjects to hunt celestial creatures that were so delicious.

Eliah is terribly shaken. He can't even responds to Ardax's words, which are melting in his loss. But he feels something that none of the celestial creatures is able to name. It is grief, anger, and sadness but also hatred and he is driven by a desire for revenge. Ardax is attempting to calm him down but without much of a success, Eliah is not listening. Ilemis is crying as if she knows what has just happened to her mother. The entire celestial world is upside down and grieving queen Ameris, deeply in love with Ardax, is trying to understand what they have just witnessed and explain the others who has just attacked them. Who is that creature they have never seen before? Ardax knows this is just the beginning. He asks the others to be careful.

Not much time passed, and the celestial creatures were under the attack again. This time it was a very destructive one, when an exceptionally large group was killed. And the attacks gradually escalated. But the celestial creatures are adaptable and learn very quickly. Ardax literally called in an army to put this all to an end. Eliah was so blinded by anger and hatred that he forgot that Ilemis was still alive. Ites, an excellent friend of Ardax himself, started to look after her. However, his future love-to-be was supposed to be Ameris and they were to become the royal couple of the celestial creatures and unite the entire celestial kingdom. But this had been disrupted by the strikes of a terrible enemy.

Ardax decided that it would be the best to watch their enemy and learn from him to be able to defend themselves with his own weapons. He summoned young but incredibly wise Oliaf and entrusted him with this task, and Olaf was eager to get cracking. He was very slim, but agile and fast. Eliah also wanted to take part in this expedition, but Ardax immediately said it was out of the question. However, he called for another man, his best friend and main advisor Aras. Aras was very capable and smart, and he could handle any situation. Finally, they were joined by another person – his close female friend Xetis. These four set out on a very menacing mission into the places where none of the celestial creatures would ever dare to go. Everyone was afraid of the dark depths, and they knew why. On the other hand, it was vital to study their enemy and learn from him to defeat him once and for all. The expedition was diving into very dark depths. Ardax knew why he had decided to take Oliaf with him. Oliaf was one of the few who could feel the danger and avoid it.

The celestial creatures had various abilities and skills they were just beginning to understand. They were diving deeper and deeper into the ocean, encountering the enemies who were extremely far and getting ready for a hunt. They were well organized and Eld was preparing his group for the fight with their available weapons. The celestial beings were studying their behavior and they noticed also other kinds of predators. They found out that the dark world was much more complex and interesting. All the time they were watching the enemies hunt and cooperate, and they found some of their weaknesses and the way how to protect themselves from these predators.

Ameris was overjoyed when she met Ardax after he had come back. She wondered why he had left her out of the expedition, but Ardax didn't hesitate a moment, he kissed Ameris and reassured her he had just wanted to keep her safe. The celestial creatures began to get ready. Eliah, recovered but still broken with a scar on his heart, was also training with the first army that Ardax and Aras had put up for a great battle against the predators. Aching Eliah took this preparation very seriously. All of them worked hard to be able to face these predators. Oliaf, who was leading the reconnaissance service of the celestial beings, had already seen that the predators were about to attack the celestial world again. But this time everyone was ready, and they had set a trap for the enemy. The shark creatures with Eld at the helm had no inkling that they had been tricked and, as always, went for prey. Eld might have had a kind of hunch, but he decided to ignore it and it was a mistake. They attacked the bait, consisting of nothing else but the puppets that did not taste good. It was a bitter experience because Eliah and other celestial warriors struck very quickly and began slaughtering them. Ardax, Aras, Ameris, Eliah and other warriors were prevailing, defeating a small group of predators in a highly organized manner. Eld was taken aback but reacted very promptly and managed to kill some warriors. Zealous Eliah wanted to chase Eld, but he escaped very quickly on the shark. Eliah watched him for a moment, but Ardax followed them, preventing Eliah from swimming any further. However, Eliah managed to hit the shark on which Eld was riding with a spear, and blood some blood spilled, and Eliah took a few sips.

As soon as he had done so, something inside him started changing. It was his structure.

7

Eliah turned into something that scared Ardax and the others. Suddenly he had very sharp and terrifying teeth, as sharp as razorblades, able to cut anything. He became a hybrid. He was drawing the energy from the sun and water itself would be enough for him, but he also had a stomach now, together with other organs necessary for its functioning. When Eliah recovered from the transformation, he was in a good mood. Ardax, on the other hand, was very surprised and anxious about what had happened to his brother. Eliah was very nice to his brother and all his loved ones, but he said he had to become independent. He would like to set up an army and fight against the shark species. Ardax and others didn't like this idea but there was nothing they could do. They couldn't stop him so they agreed they would support him in this war against the predators. Ameris had no objections, because she wanted to unite the celestial world by her union with Ardax and she desired to wear the Queen's crown and stand by Ardax. However, Ardax now did not want to take such a responsibility, considering the problems with his brother.

Over time, Eliah formed a group that undertook extremely dangerous expeditions whose purpose was to hunt the predators. They killed one after the other, and gradually they all turned into hybrids. When Alegon found out, he summoned Eld. Only now did he learn that Eld had invaded the celestial world. It infuriated him and ordered Eld to fix it. Desperate Eld knew he needed a strong army. Eliah's expeditions played into his hands, so he began to build the army, too. However, it was a difficult task. The predators at the time were quite self-sufficient and everyone wanted to rule. Eliah's army was also still growing and killing the predators. After quite a long time, Ardax and Eliah met. He was very delighted to be able to greet his brother. But he was different, his skin colour changed to darker, probably because he had spent a lot of time in the dark depths. However, Eliah had a good reason to meet with Ardax. He asked him for help. He knew a great war was coming so he asked Ardax for a large army. The predators were uniting because of Eliah and his already vast army. Ardax wanted to support his brother in this war despite his own doubts very much, and he knew his grief, so he offered to help him. But they also needed other support, namely support from Ameris, who did not approve of the war. Yet one event convinced her - the coronation and the union with Ardax. She knew the war would grant her this opportunity.

The celestial army began to unite, and a huge army of men and no longer underestimated women was formed. Ameris was a quick learner and she inspired other women who became good and agile fighters. That was the strength of the celestial army. As for the composition, it did not know any restrictions. The preparation was excellent, there were also improvements by Ameris alone and other female fighters. They invented various effective weapons, because although the spear was good, it was quite clumsy. They managed to reduce their weapons in size, and they could also be used to cut. They were the first sword-like cutting weapons. It was simply admirable how those creatures evolved, whether intellectually or technologically. They were underwater creatures, unable to survive above the ocean yet, but the ocean mountains were their home, which they needed to protect. Eld also set up an army, but it lacked the unity. He had the Alegon's support, but it was also quite uncertain. Feriases were well organized, but not good warriors. They were dangerous and strong, but their tactics and experience were weak.

The army of rookies marched upward along the rock rising to the surface. It was a huge mountain of all mountains and was home not only to the predators but also the celestial creatures. One of them lived at the foot of the oceanic mountains and others on their very peak. But now came the time to decide on the rule over these very nourishing sub-oceanic mountains. Two armies, which had been watching each other from the distance, met face to face. They were still primitive armies but determined to fight. Unexpectedly, a new creature entered this battle, and the shark creatures hadn't seen this coming. It had been created by a short evolution of hybrids and they were the dolphin creatures. It was what Eliah called himself too, because he was of a similar structure and thus, he bred a being that would help them in the fight against the shark creatures. The shark creatures were pretty much afraid of them. The thing was that they must have posed the greatest threat to the celestial army, and when the celestials deployed such a powerful weapon against them, and now the result of the fight played more into the hands of the celestial creatures. However, the shark creatures did not know any fear and were very brutal warriors, so they should not have been underestimated. They met at the interface of the depths not far from the ocean surface. For both sides, this position was unfavorable, but the centre is the centre and both armies wanted the same thing, their space. The predators wanted even more; they needed food if they were to survive. Therefore, they also needed to control the territory, and the celestial creatures were in their way.

They didn't communicate, they were just looking at each other from the safe distance. The negotiations were unnecessary. What is more, there was also a language barrier. Their minds didn't think alike and both sides knew it would be useless. Respect held them back for a while but finally all that anger and hatred gave them courage to fight. Eld didn't want to wait any longer and Eliah was impatient. They attacked each other violently. Ameris and Ardax only watched these two groups. They hit each other like two waves coming from two different worlds. You could see nothing but flying limbs of some predators who gave up very quickly. They were weak allies and it made Eld furious, and he stabbed one warrior after another. Soon Eld and Eliah came across each other. They were fighting for quite a long moment and Eliah, driven by his anger and determination to take revenge, almost cut Eld's body in half. Eld screamed in pain and Eliah tried to finish him, but Rehat, the lord of Feriases, came to Eld's rescue. He threw a spear at Eliah, who managed to avoid being hit, but the spear yet scraped his face. Eld took advantage of this and immediately ran away, suppressing the pain with only strong will. At that moment, the entire predatory army took to flight. Eliah tried to pursue his enemy, but Ardax and the other friends stopped him. Eliah didn't like it, but Ardax knew why he was doing it. There was a great power lurking in the depths that would surely kill Eliah and the whole army.

All of them returned to their kingdom on the top of the sub-oceanic mountain. A lot of the celestial beings were still in the shock from the battle. Eliah was angry with his brother. He had expected much more from this fight and blamed his brother for making a huge mistake when he had stopped him and prevented him from chasing the predators. Ardax tried to explain him that the depths were hiding much bigger and frightening secrets, and they were not ready to fight them yet. It was pointless. Ameris believed that Ardax would finally accept the coronation and their union, but she was disappointed again. Ardax confessed he didn't love Ameris. He was in love with Xetis who was already pregnant with their child. Ameris was dismayed and upset. Ardax decided to leave the mountains and find the shelter somewhere else. He discovered a small sub-oceanic mountain far away from home and the small band led by Ardax settled down there and this place became the base of the kingdom of Asads.

As time passed, a lot of down-hearted creatures broke their alliances and again joined their forces. Ameris united nine kingdoms into a new one. They built up a huge barrier from stones. It looked like giant cobwebs all around and prevented the predators from penetrating inside. The hybrids were assigned to a particularly important task – to protect the celestial world from the predators. Eliah's kingdom resided in these stone cobwebs and protected the celestial kingdom. They became the guards of the celestial kingdom.

8.

Asads settled down far from the world where all the suffering had started. Ardax's beautiful child was born. He was holding the baby in his arms and enjoying the magical moments and yet thinking about one thing. A lot of kingdoms which were already living their varied and wonderful lives had emerged and yet they were still afraid of the enemy lurking in the unknown depths. The attacks of the predators didn't cease but so many kingdoms and various lives had emerged, that the raids were less and less intense. Furthermore, even the predators themselves were not united and fought against each other. Nature played a very strange game that helped to develop the life in this paradise. However, we need to bear in our minds that one king had survived this battle, the king able to unite all kingdoms to form one and it could be the end of good old times for the celestial creatures who would definitely attempt to stop him. So Ardax, the king of Asads, could enjoy spending time with his child.

These creatures were gorgeous in a way. They had beautiful faces with small and a bit bulging mouths and lovely shaped eyes. Instead of hair they had just small lumps decorating their heads in stripes and their ears were only slightly developed, looking more like small scars on both sides of their skulls. Their figures were amazing, they were tall and slim, they had a green skin whose color usually changed depending on the environment. Th membranes among the fingers and toes enabled them to swim well and fast. All these features made it hard for the predators to catch them. Their limbs always regenerated but losing them hurt very much. You would think they were immortal, but it was quite the opposite – they were very fragile. The abdominal and chest injuries were terminal. Also, when they lost their heads, it was a certain death. And over time, these peaceful creatures gained various abilities. They were highly creative, they constructed dwellings bordered by large rocky walls on the top of a mountain, where they built a cobweb-like roof of an unknown material in the shape of an umbrella, which protected these creatures from above. Like many other kingdoms, they strategically occupied one mountain and could mine the material, which they used to make weapons and other useful things. Of course, since they lived in water, they did not know fire. Nevertheless, these creatures were so advanced that they were able to build and mine in a form that was most convenient for them. Therefore, even their weapons were carved. So, given the existing conditions, they were armed very well, but whenever a group of predators attacked, there were some casualties. It was not that they were defeated, in the end, the predators had other, easier prey to hunt. They were the autotrophic living beings, and they drew their energy from the starlight. They also discovered a technology that provided them with the power of light even in the darkness therefore they were able to take trips into the depths, even though just for a limited time.

The proud leader of Asads was still holding his child up in the air. They named the baby Tehas, which meant „the chosen one“ in their language. King Ardax called out in front of everyone: "This is our future which will change the entire world!" Everybody started swimming happily around him in a circle, celebrating the birth of a new descendant of this group. It was a lovely party. Asads began hopping, which in water meant floating, performing nice acrobatic stunts, somersaults or just showing their combat skills they used in the battles against the predators. When the days of the celebration were over, the calm and quiet life was restored again in this small underwater world. The king was very smart and wanted all his beings to be the same. The creatures who came into this world didn't have to work very hard because they would learn everything from the beings who had already experienced quite a lot here. The king was walking through his kingdom where these creatures were living their happy lives. They were admired by both Ardax and his queen Xetis who were showing little Tehas the world into which he had been born. "What do you think, my dear, will our son live a long and beautiful life?" asked Xetis and Ardax just smiled: "I sincerely hope so. And not only that, but he will also change this world for the better." Xetis was full of doubts. "Do you really think so?" Ardax looked deep into her eyes, but she just shook her head. "If you believe it so firmly, I will believe it too." Although she was beset by doubts, she stood by his side and supported him. Their close friends Aras and Hetes and their two children were just walking up to them. They greeted each other warmly, as usual. "We are very pleased to see you, my lord." "Pleasure is all ours, dear friends." They both took a bow and Ardax and Xetis did the same. "You were rewarded with a dazzling child. I can see that our kingdom is growing into great beauty," Aras admired the royal offspring. In return, Ardax repeated out of decency: "You also got a beautiful child. Your family enriches our kingdom, and I am delighted that together we can develop our marvelous world." "Well, I'd love to say that's true, but we all know that these moments are always temporary." "Stop it. Don't spoil our king and queen's joyful moment," Hetes interrupted him to ease the tension. "It is okay, my dear Hetes, your partner is right. There are tough times ahead of us and they will surely come from over there," said Xetis and she pointed into the darkness behind the wall, making their two friends even more frightened. But then Ardax intervened as he could no longer bear those negative attitudes evoking fear of a bad future. "Come on, stop it, my dear!" Everyone was suddenly quiet, waiting for what Ardax was about to say. "Yes, there is a great danger lurking in the depths. But that doesn't mean there's nothing we can do about it. We must realize that it is our responsibility to prepare our offsprings for all this. It may seem like we are stuck here forever, in this small space, but believe me, if we train our future generation well, they will eventually change this unpleasant situation. After all, look at those young people over there," he points to a small group of young Asads who are fencing tenaciously, learning to fight and entertaining other groups, playing various roles and engaging in fighting, while other groups of Asads are making up other tasks and traps for them and they are also having a good time. "See? Everything is still being prepared, there are more and more of us and let's not forget our friends from other kingdoms. Yes, we haven't seen them for ages, but that doesn't mean we will never see them again." "I shall point out - and you must agree - that our spies are coming home less and less frequently. How long have they been gone now?" Aras worries. Ardax nods in agreement, but at the same time reminds him of one thing. "You are right, Aras, my friend, but you heard that last time they dared go much deeper. They are facing different threats there, but they have also found other peaceful creatures. And it gives us hope that there will be more and more such predators. That's the positive side of the matter." Aras agrees but Hetes and Xetis join the conversation: "Let's talk about something else, shall we?"

And suddenly, with a great rumble, signals usually given by their spies, begin to come. Everyone is immediately startled, and the creatures take their positions to defend the border set by the great wall. There are no gates because you can swim over the wall. Of course, the wall is protected by various effective weapons that they managed to develop. Ardax and Aras send their loved ones and children to safety straight away, while they quickly put on their armor and accompanied by a very strong army, they are mounting to the top of the wall, where they have picked up a signal from. All at once they can see a small group of predators chasing their spies. At Ardax's command, they launch the powerful arrows that could stab the enemy hard. The arrows are rolling like torpedoes at the predators, who abruptly withdraw and retreat. A small group of spies, using cute dolphins as a means of transport, is ascending to the top of the big wall surrounded by a large cobweb.

9

The predators are prevailing, thanks to their strength and typical resourcefulness. They are also famous for their fighting skills as this skill is rooted in their subconsciousness. They are particularly good at overcoming fears. So good that it might seem they don't know what fear is. (That's the reason why the celestial creatures are so afraid of them. However, they are also learning how to tackle their fear, although there is a long way to go for them yet and the predators are one step ahead.) Moreover, they have the strategical abilities necessary to fight or occupy any territory convenient for them. They also took control over various mountains, from which they can carve various effective weapons, as well as dwellings. Although they don't establish the borders on their territories, they have miscellaneous temporary walls. However, something is still wrong with their perfection. It is their disunity, which makes them very vulnerable. Therefore, the strongest and largest shark kingdom by size is already considering how to unite all predators. There are other, though not so strong, kingdoms competing with the shark kingdom, which they call Ariads. Its leader is Eld Ion. He is a tyrant, and he conquered several tribes of the peaceful creatures, the heterotrophic living beings, kept in the reservations by Ariads who thus secure a relatively unlimited amount of food for them. Many kingdoms have failed to do this. Most are just doomed to hunt free primitive creatures, and this does not guarantee a stable supply of food needed for the long-term development of a kingdom such as the kingdom of Ariads. And yet Ariads still hunt the random creatures and the predators that compete with them. It is this struggle among predators that gives a great chance for the development.

Eld Ion, the leader of Ariads, is trying to figure out how to seize the territories of the peaceful creatures and the predators. It costs him a lot of energy and brave warriors whom he could trust. He is working on a plan to solve this problem. He knows it will be hard. Furthermore, his son was born, and this tethers him to his home and gives the several kingdoms who have betrayed him in the battle, the opportunity to mobilize and develop into greater perfection in the fight and strategy. So, it happened that one king has to attack and seize another territory and it is not going to be a piece of cake. His son Lex Ion has grown up a little. Now he is training with other warriors, and he likes it very much. He is growing up fast and learning to hunt and although there is still a lot to master, he is improving. After all, he is growing up among the best of the best predators. Right now, he is fighting with one of his peers who is also his very good friend. Et Isel is standing opposite Lex, and they are practicing the fight with sticks. Both can use the water for different stunts. The laws applicable at the bottom of the sea are remarkably interesting if you can use them to your advantage. And nothing can stop the creatures from using these laws in combat. They are both showing off, they are still young, but already well developed, they just need more experience. Although their figures are slightly smaller than those of celestial creatures, they are much faster, more agile, and currently even stronger. Their skin also changes its color according to the environment, but the basic one is darker blue, alternately with red stripes. They look like semi-sharks that have two legs and hands with membranes among the toes, with a better shaped face with very sharp and prominent teeth. They are not ugly creatures, and they could not be classified as beautiful either, certainly not, but they have their advantages. Although the celestial creatures are more beautiful, Ariads have already managed to outdo the sharks in terms of development and appearance.

The two young Ariads are fighting hard. They are being watched by Eld Ion himself. Eld Ion is enormously proud of his offspring and the way how he is fighting with his friend. Telepathic communication is a matter of course, how else could they communicate on the seabed? And they do not yet know a world other than water. Et Isel is brandishing a stick. He's a bit shorter, but a little faster while Lex is stronger, which can be a big advantage in combat. "Well, you little brat? Will you finally show me something, or will you just be waving a stick here?" Lex is smiling at Et who keeps swinging his stick. Lex is dodging him, covering his blows. "And when will you ever show something? You fucking wretch!" They are both smiling and poking fun at each other to distract the opponent. They are performing acrobatic stunts, fencing with the sticks, avoiding each other's attacks. "So, you're saying I'm a wretch? I will show you who is the wretch here!" He decides to attack Et hard. Et is trying to soften the blow, but he fails because Lex is a little smarter. He is using his strength and agility, he pushes on Et and hits his body, and this is the end of the training fight with the sticks. Everyone bursts into laughter and the two friends telepathically show respect to each other. "I am very glad that we two had a chance to fight and I admit the defeat. You're good." Lex puts his arm around Et's shoulders. "Come on, Et, you really believed you could beat me? Well, I love you anyway, so I accept your defeat." "You do? Excellent, but next time I'll beat you, trust me." "Not even in your wildest dreams, my dear friend." "Oh, Lex, you'll never

change, your self-confidence will be the death of you, mind me, and I will
be the only one able to save you." "Hmm, looks like I am the lucky one to
have you by my side. How on earth would I cope without you?" "That's
what I've been asking myself too." They start laughing when out of the
blue Eld Ion himself and Et's father appear right in front of them, with
their hands behind their backs and severe looks in their eyes. "My lord,"
Et greets the king humbly and Lex just smiles at his strict father. "Well,
well, you should be the example of how to treat the elders. Hello, Et. I am
glad you are a good friend of my disobedient and unscrupulous son Lex."
"Come on, father, stop it." "And what is more, he is always talking back.
See, Et? Never treat anyone this way." "Why are you scaring him, Dad?"
"I am not scaring anyone, I am just teaching our future generation,
where you belong to as well, how to treat the elders." "I am afraid I don't
understand." "What don't you understand, son?" "I don't understand
how you managed to conquer such a huge territory with this kind of
attitude." They look each other in the eyes, and you could feel the great
tension between these two stubborn men with sharp teeth. Suddenly
Lex attacks his father with a stick, but it is a big mistake. It is not an
accident that Eld Ion is a famous and very strong warrior with a lot of
experience from various fights. He manages to avoid his son's attack, but
Lex immediately tries to attack Eld again. Eld immediately grabs him by
the neck and pushes him to the bottom of the sea. Suddenly, his dear
queen, Uri Ion, comes to his rescue. She is swimming fast, as fast as
a wink, she tries to push Eld away, begging him to let go of Lex. Eld
keeps pressing Lex to the ground for a bit longer and then he releases
his grasp. Lex jumps up swiftly. It is obvious he is furious with his father
but on the other hand he must show him respect as he is the leader of
a strong group. Then he gives him a shy smile. "Finally, you have proved
to be worthy to be the leader of this group. I am glad you are my father."
He hugs his father, and his father accepts this hug. Uri is happy. "For
a moment you made me truly believe you were going to kill each other."
Both turn to her and say: "Don't worry, we were just teasing each other."
"Were you? From where I was standing, it looked quite different." "I'd
never hurt my own son." "It's settled then. Let's have something to eat

now.“ “Brilliant. What are we having?“ “Our most favorite dish, of course.“ They are going home, followed by frightened Et, and they have a delicious meat specialty from their reservation they have just conquered. They are eating the meat of the peaceful creatures, imprisoned, and left to their fate, like the cattle ready to be eaten by another creatures.

For these peaceful creatures, who are thinking of nothing but how to break out of this trap, it is a scary sight.

Dolphins are creatures that have been fighting against sharks, their sworn enemy, for a very long time. Their evolution was a long process. They are very cute, but they can also be dangerous, especially when sharks appear in their territory. These battles between dolphins and sharks have a long history but now the battles have become a war led by their close allies, celestial creatures. They were the ones who discovered a tiny spark of hope for the peaceful creatures who could eventually live in peace and love. Therefore, they are doing their best to aid the kingdom of Asads.

Dolphins are able to anticipate the events that might overturn the whole war in favor of the community of the peaceful creatures. They are entering the rocky mountain of Asads and friendly greeting each other. Ardax is saying hello to the best friend of Asads, a dolphin called Hetchi, very warmly. "I love you, Hetchi..." They are rubbing their noses and smiling at each other, enjoying this lovely moment. Then Ardax salutes excellent spies from their kingdom. By the way, these spies were also something like the first diplomats. Ardax and Oliaf hug each other. "It's great to see you here again. Tell me, my dear friend, what kind of the news are you bringing from that world?" Ardax is wondering. Oliaf replies seriously: "Well, I'd love to bring you the best news ever, but I am afraid it is not as optimistic as it used to be several journeys ago." Having heard those words, Ardax's face gets pensive as well. The group is joined by the wives of both lords, Xetis and Heteh. They warmly welcome a visit that has just arrived after an exceedingly difficult expedition. They kiss on the cheeks and the dolphins are just merrily circling around. Ardax and Oliaf step back and engage in a conversation that no one can hear. "So, tell me, my friend, what is going on in the depths?" Oliaf thinks for a moment, then begins. "Well, together with our friends from another kingdom we got quite far away from our home. At first everything seemed to be all right, except it wasn't. We got caught in the middle of the fight between two groups of the strong predators and one of them was finally defeated." "That's not bad news." "Just wait, there is more," Oliaf interrupts Ardax and goes on: "This strong group isn't only trying to unite the predators, they are also attacking weaker and less protected peaceful creatures and then they leave them there." "I don't understand. Why would they do that?" wonders Ardax. Oliaf continues: "We were also wondering why, and we didn't understand, but then we figured it out. They let the peaceful creatures reproduce and they hunt the older, though not too old, group and feed on them. They let the babies be and these are then looked after by a small group of the elders. And this happens again and again." Ardax is lost in his thoughts. "That's really not good news. They're evolving and getting smarter." "So, what is on your mind, my friend?" Oliaf asks Ardax to find out what he should do next, because he's stuck and can't find a solution to the problem. Ardax is thinking, feeling almost hopeless, but in the end, something comes to his mind. "Oliaf, my friend, now it is essential that you follow me thoroughly. It will be a very difficult task, but don't worry, you will succeed. You have to set out on a big journey again, but this time you have to connect with one our old friend and enemy at the same time. This enemy is also an enemy of the predators." "You must be joking; nobody has been able to reach an agreement there." "There is no need to worry. However, you must fulfill this task, because that's the only way we can eliminate our enemy for a while." "Okay, but what shall I say to him?" Oliaf is terrified as he is waiting for what kind of a message Ardax is going to send to one of the very treacherous creatures, called the guards.

The guards are creatures feeding on the sharks. They also take the energy from the sun, and they even grow various kinds of seaweed, which the peaceful creatures envy them. But these hybrids are terribly angry with the celestial creatures now, after the last battle, therefore it will be very hard to approach them. They are called Echans and they developed from the celestial creatures. Eld Ion fought against them, and he lost because they are a lot stronger and bigger. It may be said they belong to those strongest and fittest warriors, but they are loners. Furthermore, they are of unclear character and nobody, neither the predators nor the celestial creatures, knows anything about their motives. They live separately on one vast place where they are guarding the border between the celestial world and the depths, in that huge rocky cobweb that is supposed to protect the celestials from any predators. They are a closed community which doesn't spread any further which is quite reassuring, but they still might be a threat. Eld Ion remembers very well the battle he lost, his big scar which he had got in a fight with their leader Eliah makes it impossible for him to forget. Therefore, Ardax must think carefully about the message he is going to send to his brother Eliah, the leader of the hybrids called Echans. "Listen carefully, because you must repeat exactly what I am going to say, word by word. Am I clear?" Oliaf nods and focuses on Ardax. "This is what you will tell the lord of the guards: We are the enemies of your greatest enemy; therefore, we would like to be your friends." Oliaf smiles when he hears Ardax's clever words. "I understand your message, and I will tell the lord of guards exactly what you have just told me. I sincerely hope it will work." "So do I, because we don't have many options. We can at least hope that the peace will be restored one day. I know it's a wild goose chase, but on the other hand, as I said, we don't have many options." "Well, you're right, Ardax, my friend, we don't have many options, but I believe in you."

Oliaf and Ardax rejoin the celebrations that have just begun. Everyone is happy and dancing, even though there is no music playing, it's all going on in their minds. Their senses are so developed that their telepathy also transmits sounds that only they can hear, because they are on a different frequency of telepathic communication than other creatures.

11

The big reception was hosted by the leader of Ariads, the strongest kingdom of the predators. Afterwards when they were having a rest, Eld took his son Lex aside and told him: "My dear son, listen to me very carefully. One day it will be you who will rule this kingdom and lead the great battles. Therefore, I am asking you here and now to respect me and learn from me. Our future is in your hands and once you will fight the most significant battle that will decide about the rule over all creatures in this world. My vision is to unite all the kingdoms that want to fight against us. There is one battle ahead of us now and I want you to be by my side and learn how to lead the great battles. It isn't a big kingdom, but their warriors are very skilled. We will beat them, though. You have no doubts about that, do you?" Lex only smiles. He has just become the happiest being on the planet. He has been waiting for this moment for so long, he has always desired to take part in a battle for territory. This particular territory doesn't have a strategical advantage for Eld Ion, but he wants his son to learn to fight in battles and gain the experience that will eventually help him to win the greatest fights for strategical territories. So, everyone is resting before the battle against the kingdom of Lapads.

Lapads are a small kingdom, but they have excellent warriors who aren't very fast, but they are freakishly strong. As a means of transport, they use sea lizards which look a bit like them. They hunt in a very ruthless way and endanger Ariads, although Lapads usually tend to avoid them. They know very well the legends about how they conquer kingdoms one after another, the kingdoms that betrayed them in a decisive battle. Not everyone likes what Ariads are doing, so some kingdoms are trying to unite against them.

Ariads are waking up. Eld Ion opens his eyes and wakes his beloved Uri and son Lex. Lex is very excited because he knows his big moment is coming and finally, he will be able to show his strengths and skills in a real battle. Uri doesn't like it and she asks Eld: "Don't you think it's too early?" "I don't. It's about time Lex showed what kind of a king he will be and how he will rule over my hard-won territories," replies Eld. Still feeling quite anxious, she is reluctant to let her son fight against such good warriors as Lapads are. "Don't worry, Mum, I will bring you the nicest booty you have ever seen." Uri smiles and strokes Lex's cheek. "I want nothing more than to see you come back home safe and sound, my dear son." Lex hugs her. "I promise I will be all right." "Well, it's time..." bored Eld intervenes. They both look at him with a smile and Lex follows his father out of their house. The whole army, numerous and organized, is already waiting for them. Their means of transport is sharks – blue and white, depending on their position in the society – their ravenous but loyal allies. This is the secret of Ariads' power – they have been able to tame these savage creatures. Aggression and cold-bloodedness in killing are their common features. There are also other kinds of sharks, but they are less pliable, more solitary, and therefore not especially useful in the fights. And so Eld tames his leading shark, with whom he is currently associating. When he grabs it by the nose with both palms, they are in energetic symbiosis, connected by the consciousness of both souls, they are floating in the space. After a while, Eld sits down on his white shark, with whom he has already been through various battles. Lex has tamed a young shark, which is not listening to him very much from the beginning. It is a juvenile and predatory shark that is just picking on its master. It keeps provoking him, but Lex always strikes back by hitting the shark on the mouth several times. Then the shark realizes that there are boundaries between their friendship and hatred. After this stormy exchange, Lex also gets on his shark. Eld looks concerned. "My dear son, what will become of you?" "Don't worry, father, these are just the beginnings, at one point I'll show you that I'm the king you have always wanted me to be." Eld grins. "I hope so, but I can see you still have a lot to work on. Now, please, stop showing off." And he telepathically addresses all the warriors: "There is another battle ahead of us. That kingdom isn't very large, but they do have a few very clever warriors whom we could use in our greater battles that will help us win significant wars. This fight won't be easy but if you manage to keep the formations, it will be a piece of cake. Do you understand?" They all say in unison: "We do!" "Let's go, then!" orders Eld and everyone is following him at great speed, holding their weapons and riding the sharks.

Eld Ion is leading his army into the battle against Lapads who have no idea that someone is coming to destroy them.

12

Both Ardax and Oliaf are saying goodbye, but Hetchi is the saddest. "Don't despair, my dear friend," Ardax reassures Hetchi, who is swimming around him. The others are also saying goodbye to a group of spies, hugging each other very fervently. After all, they are facing a difficult task, which is almost impossible to fulfill. Aras will accompany Oliaf. Heteh is not happy with this decision, but she has already come to terms with it. "Aras, my dear, be careful. I am so afraid that you will not return to us." Aras gently touches Heteh's head and tells her telepathically: "Don't worry, my dear Heteh, I will come back, and we will bring good news, that's my personal guarantee." "I pray so, but I'm still afraid something bad will happen to you." "Cheer up, Heteh, I'll take care of him," Oliaf says, reassuring her. Ardax also comes to say goodbye to his friend Aras. "I'm glad it's you who is going with Oliaf, you're the most experienced warrior of us all, so just make sure everyone gets back safe and sound." "Fear not, my lord, my gut tells me everything will turn out well and you know my feelings never let me down." "I know. Anyway, be alert because the predators are sneaking everywhere and you are about to undertake a journey to very treacherous places." They share a hug, the others do the same and the expedition is setting off. The purpose of this mission is to win a vague ally for a war against the predators. They wave their last goodbyes and disappear into the distance, in the currents that the dolphins are leaving behind. The eight-member expedition is thrown to the wolves lurking in the depths of the seas.

"So, they are gone," says Xetis. Heteh is upset that her loved one has left. "Don't worry, Aras is a good warrior and he will manage, trust me." Heteh looks Xetis in her eyes and replies: "Easy to say, but what would you do if your love left for such a dangerous journey?" "I'd surely worry very much, but certain decisions are necessary." Xetis is trying to calm Heteh down, but she is unable to bear it all. "My dear Heteh, they are all very experienced and Aras can handle anything. We must be strong. The war is coming, and we must be ready," Ardax is talking to everyone telepathically. They are listening to his speech and get to work immediately so they can prepare for the big war against the predators. "Oh, my dear, do you really think that the war is coming?" Ardax looks at Xetis who is reluctant to believe that the battle which will decide the fate of this world is so close. Ardax strokes Xetis's head. "Xetis, my dear, I am sure of it. What was a long time ago was just the beginning. We all have to be ready, because our enemy is mobilizing, he is getting better and stronger every moment and with every single little battle, so, dear Xetis and Heteh, you have to start preparing for the battle and stop despairing and hesitating." Then he kisses Xetis and they join the others to prepare for the war. All of them are training in combat with various tools and weapons, like a monolithic cell.

An unpleasant surprise is awaiting the predators when they encounter this strong resistance in the decisive battle over what life will prevail in this paradise.

13

Lapads are giants with huge hairless heads lined with the stripes of scars also reaching their necks, red skin, and few big sharp teeth. Their limbs are enormous and strong, with the membranes among their fingers. They are riding ugly, sizeable, blue-skinned lizards with long tails and they are hunting randomly. They know no boundaries and don't respect any rules, therefore they are vague. And these creatures are about to be attacked by Ariads. Lapads have been avoiding Ariads for ages but now they have crossed the line and Ariads can't put up with it any longer. Lapads are looting the conquered reservations full of the peaceful creatures that provide Ariads with the constant and endless source of food. Lapads are also doing other damage. When Ariads came to pick their kill, Lapads attacked them and slaughtered them one by one. Then Eld and his group lost their patience, saying that they would end Lapads, who do more harm to the predators than they help, once and for all.

They are hurtling on the predatory sharks, which are already hungry for the fight, and they can't wait to hunt their prey, but Eld and his party are still holding them back. Lapads are re-entering the reservations of the peaceful creatures and devouring everything in their way. Ariads stop for a moment, their sharks fidgeting impatiently, but Eld is just watching Lapads. His son Lex addresses him. "My father, what is going on? What are we waiting for?" Eld just keeps looking at the unsuspecting Lapads peacefully disrupting Ariads' space. "The time of the battle has not yet come. We have to be patient and wait for the right moment." "For the right moment? And you will know when the right time comes?" Lex looks at him in surprise, but his father is still waiting patiently. Lapads jump after another prey when out of the blue, they are under a surprising attack. Huge spears are raining down on them in the depths of the sea. Eld issues an order, and everyone dives down to the depths with great vigor and Lapads are experiencing a storm. But this is not any storm, it is the storm called Ariads and it is bringing them death. They are struck by large spears and are attacked by a mighty army raging with hatred. Those who have successfully avoided the spears are going to have to fight their enemy face to face. The sharks are aggressively biting into their prey and the warriors are slashing decimated Lapads with their sharp weapons. Lex is enjoying the fight, and he is killing one Lapad after another as if it were a game. Eld is proudly watching his son fight. He is satisfied now, because he knows that his son will be a great warrior and king who will rule over all predators. Lapads do not even have a chance to escape, because they have walked into the trap of a large reservation belonging to Ariads and they have no mercy on anyone who robs them of their catches and territories. The lizards also fall victim, losing their heads and limbs. Ariads are excited, they are going to be well fed, they are going to eat their enemies alive.

Majority of Lapads are dead very soon and those who survive, fall into captivity. Only blood is spreading in the sea, it can be smelt from the distance. It's a warning sign for anyone who would dare to oppose Ariads. If they violate their territory, they will pay the ultimate price.

Ariads begin to celebrate after they have killed other merciful beings who happened to be in the wrong place at the wrong time. All this is watched by other creatures who have just witnessed the massacre. They have seen the fall of one of the species, but it doesn't matter. It's always good when the predators kill each other. However, they feel also sad because some lenient innocent beings have been killed as well in this fight for power. After this victorious fight, Ariads are coming home with their booty. The settlers are welcoming them warmly and they are celebrating. The warriors are being celebrated as great heroes who have won the battle but not yet the war. That one is still waiting for them and Eld knows that too, so now he is enjoying the victory very carefully. He looks at his son and he can already see the future; he can see how Lex will rule the great kingdom of Ariads one day.

Lapad survivors and their lizards have become the prisoners and allies at the same time but tied to the chains like some beasts.

14

Aras, Oliaf and Hetchi are in a hurry, the other five companions struggling to keep up with them. They are pursuing their destiny, chasing after their future and former ally. At least they hope they will be able to persuade the guards. It is a very uncertain path, but the only way how to defeat the predators. Suddenly Aras stops abruptly and hides behind the stone, the others following his example. It was a very narrow escape from the danger awaiting them in the far and making the celestial beings scared. They might be resistant to fear but there is still a lot to learn in the field of killing. Aras is looking around in an attempt to find out what is happening, and he can see big creatures sitting on the lizards and eating up defenseless peaceful beings. "Oh, this is not good," murmurs Aras. The others are just watching and wondering what is not good. "Oliaf, you said that one species owns another, either predators or peaceful beings." "Right," Oliaf is not sure why Aras is asking. "So, who does this peaceful species belong to?" Oliaf peeks out carefully, but he also returns behind the stone quickly, frightened and nervous. "Don't worry, Oliaf, everything will be all right." "No, it won't. We should vanish pretty fast because it will go awry here in a moment." Aras grabs Oliaf by his hand and stops him from doing something stupid or panic. And suddenly there is a great wave of predators rolling, who are cutting everything that is standing in their way, right in front of the eyes of the celestial creatures. Oliaf is trembling from fear and doesn't know what to do. Fortunately, Aras is by his side and knows very well how to act in situations like this. Oliaf has already been through a lot, but he still finds it hard to get used to this. Other companions are also not sure what to do, so they are following Aras's example and orders. They can see the terror, the predators cutting each other in half, also hurting the peaceful creatures which are both victims and prey in this massacre. After a while, everything calms down. Aras understands now is the right time to disappear and he beckons the others to follow him. They are taking a detour to see what Eld Ion, and his tribe can accomplish.

Aras and the others are once again on dangerous paths when they come across a small group of brave peaceful creatures who look like little elves with big eyes and ears. Little elves with dark green skin and brown braids that adorn their bodies. Of course, they do not welcome Aras's group in any peaceful way. They attack them, but mighty Aras hits the strongest one hard, knocks the other one down and the rest of them are hesitant about what to do next. Then Aras says, "Stop, stop messing with us, aren't we on the same side?" The peaceful beings stop fighting and think about Aras's question. Then one of them comes forward. "I'm sorry for the misunderstanding, but we're just wanderers and survivors after everything the predators have done to us." "See? That's why we are following our destiny. We're looking for reinforcements for a decisive battle that would turn everything around." "Decisive battle? Now it is getting interesting. Talk, my friend, for you are the enemy of our enemy." Aras looks around, glances at the group, and smiles before saying anything telepathically. "Our king sent us to win one very strong ally, but that ally is not our great friend. I know, I know, you're confused now, but it is okay. The ally I am talking about is the guards." "What?" Everyone shakes their heads in disbelief. "I know, it's crazy, but they're the only ones who have defeated the strongest group of predators in one battle, who want to control everything, and they also want to keep us as a constant supply of food." The merciful wanderers are still shaking their heads, but in the end, they come to terms with it and after a short telepathic debate they make their decision. "Well, after a minor disagreement, we finally concluded that nothing matters anymore. We have no choice, it's our only chance, so we chose to join you and help you get to the guards." The faces of Aras, Oliaf, and Hetchi are glowing, they know that they could use any reinforcements now. "Then let's follow our destiny!" Aras commands, and they embark on a journey to find their potential ally. They are running down the perilous alleys between rocks, trying to avoid various predators lurking for their prey. Some in small groups, others are as loners. However, none of them is less dangerous, because even loners can do a lot of damage. They are more dangerous than those small groups, because they are very strong and nothing limits them, they can kill any creature without blinking the eye. Because they are loners, every prey is unbelievably valuable to them. The wanderers are sailing carefully, avoiding the danger, and are already approaching their destination. Suddenly, Aras stops them with a hand gesture, and Oliaf, who has brought them here, is watching the stone cobweb in the distance.

They feel horrified when they are looking at the pen that the celestial creatures have built to protect them from the murderous predators.

15

Eld is walking slowly and quietly alongside his son, and he feels satisfied and immensely proud of his offspring. "My son, you have fought very bravely today but there's still a lot to learn." Lex looks at his father and there is a sign of anger in his eyes but it's all because he is young, and his pride blinds him. But that will change, life will teach him a lesson. Eld knows that very well, he knows the bitter taste of defeat, he knows what it is like to lose just because of being too proud and self-confident. He touches the scar on his chest, and he clearly remembers the fight against the hybrid whose name he can't even remember. However, the name is written in his subconsciousness forever. And the name is Eliah. Eliah is the one who defeated Eld Ion, and he will never forget it. "Lex, my only son, there is one rule you have to bear in your mind till the end of times: Never underestimate anyone for if you do that, it might cost you your life." He strokes his son's head and Lex is humbly listening to his father's advice. "Don't worry, father, one day you will be proud of me. I will defeat your enemy you talk about so often." Eld's blood is up immediately, and he replies angrily: "You need to forget about Eliah. He is my problem, not yours. Promise me, Lex, whatever may happen, you will always listen to me even though you might not like it. Promise me," insists Eld Ion. "Okay, father, I promise that I will always listen to you." "That's settled then," Eld hugs his son. It's almost incredible how much these cruel creatures can love each other. Ariads can't hide this love just like they can't hide their sharp teeth. "Now it's time for another lesson and this time it will be the art of combat." He takes his training weapon and asks his son to do the same.

Eld and Lex are beginning to fight with such fervor that no one can cross their path now without getting hurt.

16

Aras has been looking at the cobweb for some time now, trying to figure out how to approach it and contact the guards without being cut into pieces. "What do you say, my friend? How are we going to get inside?" Oliaf asks Aras and interrupts his thoughts. Aras looks furiously at Oliaf but Hetchi is calming down the situation with his friendly manners. He has been on so many dangerous journeys that he doesn't know how to treat his friends when they are thinking about something important. Aras is about to utter a few words when he glances something in the distance. He is not sure what he is looking at, but he knows it's already too late. The guards are very fast, and they are with them in a second. They are immediately surrounded, all the spears aimed at them. "What the hell are you doing here, you buggers?" the voice is screaming in their minds, that voice which would rather kill than talk to some bastards. Aras knows he needs to think carefully about what he is going to say. But the thoughts are sometimes faster than words. "We are coming in peace!" he says slowly, not to make the matters worse but they can hear the cruel laughter in their minds. "That's what everybody says." "Well, the difference is, we really mean that," answers Aras in a friendly manner to hold his thoughts together so that the guards aren't able to read them. "I am going to ask you again, what are you doing here?" "We, humble creatures, have come to ask for a piece of advice." The insidious laughter starts again. When it stops, the voice says: "We are at our own wits' end, how on earth could we be of any help?" Aras is thinking and trying to identify the creature that is talking to him. But he is hidden very well, to be safe from any possible peril. All creatures have developed the ability to sense other creature's intentions since they can communicate telepathically. "It's not exactly a piece of advice we are asking you for, it's a kind of help." That insidious laughter again. "It's amazing how naive you are, expecting help you will never get, you can never get. Go back home." "But we also have a message for you. The message from our king, your brother," intervenes Oliaf who is a very skilled negotiator and communication is his forte, although when it comes to the fight, he is a coward. The guards begin laughing again, but this time it sounds milder and more serious. "Of course, in the entire world there is just one lunatic mad enough to send me such a message, and that lunatic is my brother. Ok, I am all ears. But heaven help you if your message is unacceptable for us, strong and noble creatures." Oliaf swallows, and the message is scraping its way out of his memory. "That message, my lord, is only for you: The enemy of our enemy is our friend." A great laugh begins again, but this time it is a joyous laughter that resonates in their minds.

Eliah emerges from behind the large army of spears, aimed at the whole group of celestial beings. He is coming straight to frightened Oliaf. He is taller and more robust. His brownish, alternately rippled blue color only beautifies his skin. His eyes burning like fire evoke fear in everyone who looks into them, the slightly bumpy shapes on his head are his ornaments instead of the hair that these beings do not yet have. Eliah is staring into Oliaf's eyes, but here Aras joins in and stands between them. Eliah doesn't like it, he hisses at Aras, but he doesn't just get intimidated so easily. "What kind of creature is he who dares to deny my right to speak to a subject?" With a slight smirk on his face, Aras looks straight into those scary eyes and replies coldly: "Only the one who protects the rights of weaker creatures and is willing to die for it." Eliah's insidious laughter echoes in everyone's minds, but after a while everything falls silent. "So, I shall give these visitors a warm welcome." Everyone is surprised at first and then immediately relieved and Eliah shakes hands with Aras as a sign of friendship. After a while, they hug warmly like brothers. Oliaf is just staring blankly, not quite sure what is going on when Hetchi and the other wanderers join them and are warmly embracing everyone.

Hetchi is circling around merrily, feeling happy about the reunion of these friends.

17

Two guys are fighting, one is hitting the other and they are delighted about this simulation of a fight. Lex is trying out one special technique while Eld is just smiling and covering his son's aggressively looking blows. "Take it easy, Lex, stop focusing on the fact that you actually want to hit me." Lex still doesn't understand, and he is stubbornly attempting to strike his father with a stick, who finally shows his son how to use it simply and effectively. He hits him so hard that all Lex can do is touch his aching ankle. "See, son, even this little is enough to knock down your enemy. Remember, your strike doesn't have to be mortal, it is enough to paralyze your opponent. You can finish him later." Lex doesn't like this, but he knows his father is right. You don't need to be perfect, all you need is to be effective. And who could be a better teacher of combat than Eld Ion, the king of Ariads, himself? Lex stands up and he is trying again, this time being more cautious. He focuses also on defense. His strikes are more effective, the is trying to hit the bottom or upper part of the body, but Eld is very experienced, and he can predict his son's moves. He leaves some places unprotected, wondering whether his son will notice, but Lex is still just a beginner. Eld is aware of this, but he must punish Lex for his mistakes and teach him that he needs to take the advantage of his opponent's errors. So, he lures him onto himself and hits him in the head with a stick from behind his back, slightly but effectively. All that Lex can feel now is pain. "See, my dear son, this is how it ends up when your concentration is poor. You are hard-headed and too blinded with an idea of defeating me and that's what betrays and distracts you. Stop thinking, just imagine how you can beat me and then get it out of your head and focus just on the fight." Lex considers his father's words and all of sudden it dawns on him. He obeys his father because who else could be right if not him, who is the king of Ariads, the most powerful predators. Lex is thinking again, imagining how he is defeating his father in the fight. Then he gets it out of his head, prepares for the duel, takes the combat posture and now Eld can see that his son is ready to fight. He takes his fighting stance too. They are exchanging one strike with a stick after another. They are using different combinations of hits until finally Eld stops trying so hard to let his son win this time. He wants to give him a little self-confidence, because it is self-confidence that adds to his courage and shows the warrior that anything is possible. Lex notices his father's mistake; he dodges his blow and hits him into his ribs. Eld moans a little in his mind because it really hurts. Lex smiles and Eld smiles back. "See, Lex, when you listen to me carefully, you can prove the impossible." Lex smiles at his father again: "Thank you, father, you are the greatest teacher of combat I have ever known."

As a sign of respect, they both bow. On their way home, they are engaged in a cheerful talk.

18

Everybody is dancing, hugging and having fun, just Aras and Eliah are sitting on their thrones and watching the cheering crowd. "The look at those unaware creatures makes me so sad," Eliah tells Aras telepathically. "I also feel sorrowful when I see all that tyranny in the world." Eliah is staring into the space coldly, enjoying the moment of comfort that is surrounding him. "You know, brother, you want to lead the war against something that cannot be defeated." Aras is taken aback and sort of resentful. Eliah knows very well what this war is about, it was him who wanted it most, although it was because of his hatred for one creature. "Brother, if we don't fight, we will keep dying." Eliah bursts into laughter. "Brother, we will be fighting for our lives and dying forever." Aras looks at Eliah indignantly again. He can't understand his arguments but most probably Eliah is just testing him, he wants to know how truthful he is to his opinions. "What do you suggest that we do, Eliah, the king of revenge and brother of the king who is my friend? You started this war." "Brother, it wasn't such a long time ago when we were attacked by a numerous well-organized group of predators, cruel and ruthless warriors. I met their king, who had taken everything I loved from me, in the battle and I can assure you, he is not a weak fighter." Aras is interested, and he asks: "And where is that warrior buried?" Eliah is laughing. "He isn't buried anywhere, he managed to escape eventually when I was about to finish him. His army is organized, and we can expect him to come back much stronger this time." Aras is beside himself after Eliah's words and he asks carefully: "What exactly are you expecting?" Eliah grins. "I am expecting the decisive battle on our territory. Therefore, I suggest that we should concentrate our forces here and build up the strongest army possible. Because when they come, they will be extremely powerful and united. We need to be prepared." Aras believes that the war has already begun. The decisive battle for this world is round the corner, much closer than any celestial beings would think. He drew the energy from the star again, he shuddered and started: "It's time to say goodbye then. Our group must return to our king and gradually gather the army that we need to train. Our army is not very experienced, but it has one great forte – determination." Eliah starts laughing in his typical insidious way. "I believe that one day your army will be ready to face such a strong enemy. We are lucky that the predators are not united. However, it can change pretty quickly, all they need is a mighty and very cruel king who will conquer them and then they will be on his side, and they will become very strong and able to defeat us." Aras smiles for the very first time. "So that we too shall begin to unite." Eliah smiles again and hugs Aras. "Good luck, brother." Aras doesn't hesitate a moment and orders everyone who has come with him: "Time to leave, our mission here has been accomplished." Eliah grabs him and says: "One more thing. I will assign you a small group to make your crossing safer. They are my good warriors." Aras leans towards him: "Thank you very much." Eliah nods at the seven warriors who will protect the envoys on this long journey. They are all in dark outfits that adorn their beautifully shaped figures. Their bodies always adapt to the conditions of the task they are currently performing. They are all well-armed.

Aras waves goodbye and everyone waves back.

19

A huge army ready for its big war against the predators is standing by in the darkness. Eld, his son Lex and Lex's friend Et are waiting in the background for the king's command to attack. Eld is looking at the sky and a small light in which he can see its prey appears in the distance. He must let it go for now, because there is a big battle ahead, the battle against other enemies, also the predators, who would like to assume the power too. He mastered an enormously powerful weapon, a pair of Lapads who had survived, and they will be perfect for this fight. The way to the desired rule over this world is still awfully long, but this victory might be a big step forward. Eld knows it very well. Then he looks down to the side. Staring into the darkness he can feel the rage of the enemy. He raises his hand and beckons everyone to follow him. "Let's fight, let's take control over our world!" Everyone is rushing behind him on their furious sharks. They are going like greased lightning through the deep darkness into the world of the predators. Everything around is shaking and each creature living here is very scared because this is going to be a big fight that will not be brushed aside, and it will be legendary. The predators from the kingdom of Ariads are dashing forward to conquer the territory of their fearsome enemy, Datars. Datars are already waiting with their firepower. Their leader Tarat looks into the distance and sees that his great enemy, Eld Ion, and his very strong and large army are approaching his fortress fast. The fortress is massive, located in a big mountain at the bottom of the sea, in the deep darkness. In fact, everyone is dark, their skin is dark, and it looks very weird. Their heads are the heads of snakes, and they sometimes stick out their tongues just like snakes do. They also hiss like these reptiles, but they have limbs. Tarat just raises his hand and telepathically orders everyone to await further instructions.

Eld's army is sweeping forward like an avalanche, but at the last moment it stops, almost halts. It makes Tarat angry, as he was about to wave his hand and order his army to fire at the enemy. But Eld takes the wind out of his sails. The enemies are looking at each other for a while, waiting for the next move of their opponent. Finally, Eld finds courage to address his enemy. "We haven't come here as your enemy; we have come as your friends. Put down your weapons, you cowards and traitors, and surrender." Tarat is both furious and amused and so are other Datars. "Lovely, Eld. So, when you are coming as our friend, why are you dressed in armor? Or is it your tradition to pay visits armed to the teeth?" Eld laughs, joined by Ariads. "Yes, we've come here in full armor, because we knew you would not welcome us with friendly hospitality. And I can see I was right. Look at yourselves. You are also armed to the teeth." Tarat and his companions chuckle. "Well, my friend, we both know why you've come here. Everyone in this world already knows about your intentions. Do you think that if we stay only in the darkness, we will not hear about your actions?" This time Eld only smirks and signals to his army to keep waiting. He turns to his enemy again. "Yes, it's true that we fought a few battles against our comrades, but you ran away from that decisive battle like cowardly fools. Think. Only then will we be stronger if we are united and have one king and one aim." Tarat guffaws for a while and then replies: "My friend, I am more than sure that you know what my reaction will be. I won't give in to a greedy bastard like you and all your army which has come here uninvited." He orders his forces to throw some stone spears towards Eld, but he knows they will miss the target. It's just to show they are not going to surrender. They fire some shots at Eld, but they sink in the watery sand right in front of them and the ripples get to Ariads. The army starts fidgeting, trying to keep that dust off their sensitive parts on their bodies. Eld signals his army with a gesture of his hand to hold their position and addresses Tarat and his soldiers one last time. "This is your last chance to capitulate. I challenge you to a duel and if I win, I will spare the lives of your warriors. I promise." Tarat just smiles and orders his army to fire the spears as a warning. Eld understands now that this won't do without a fight, but he counted with that. They fought once side by side, but it ended in a cowardly betrayal.

The relationships have not turned into friendships and so the battle begins. With a furious expression on his face, Eld is still holding back his army with a hand gesture. He is watching Datars retreat to their fortress, where they barricade themselves so thoroughly that not even a small fish can penetrate. Eld smiles as his first counselor, Tad Opol, and son Lex approach him and they ask, "What are we going to do now?" Eld looks at them and answers with a small grin on his face. "Don't worry, I have a plan. Why do you think I needed to get a couple of Lapads? If we need to drive those little cowards out, Lapads will help us. I had a hunch they might be of use." They both look at each other and smile, delighted about the genius of the king of Ariads. Eld waves his hand and gives a mental order: "Release Lapads!" At that moment, the ground thunders, the bottom of the sea whirls in dust, and the mountain shakes. Tarat feels a kind of fear in his heart, and when his army and he look into the distance, he says to himself: "This is not good. This is not good at all. Eld, that heartless scoundrel." Well-armed Lapads on the giant saurions in the distance, draped with various rocks and clinging warriors eager to fight. The rocks hanging on their tails are properly polished and razor sharp and they could cut any creature into pieces. Eight giant saurions are approaching, attempting to shriek but it's pointless because they are in water, on the bottom of the ocean. Datars are firing back with anything that comes into their hands but in vain. The saurions are perfectly shielded and they are listening to the cruel creatures, so they are trying to shoot at the soldier at least, but those are well protected by the rocks hanging off the saurions like shields. The army of Eld Ion is slowly and safely marching behind advancing Lapads. They are getting closer and closer, posing a threat that has no mercy on any soul living in a body of any creature in this world. Tarat is hopeless, he knows this destruction will bring his downfall. Suddenly there is a huge crash into the walls, and everything shakes terribly. And suddenly a huge crash into the walls brings a great shock. Everything begins to quake and fall, the walls are moving. They all are fleeing in front of the eyes of the creatures, they remain uncovered, defenseless. At that moment, Tarat shouts to all Datars, "Do not give up, my dear fellows, let's fight! And kill them all!"

A huge fight breaks out, spears and arrows flying here and there. The creatures on both sides are dying a cruel death. After a while, Eld and his army approach. They can only see the debris of the walls and the dust spreading all over the seabed. No one can see their hands, but Eld is resourceful. Everyone puts on a combat helmet with a kind of glass he secretly got, nobody knows from whom. They are running towards a battlefield full of chaos and they start a cruel fight. They are dying one by one. Eld and his son Et, General Tad, and a group of fighters are focusing mainly on one thing: to find Tarat, the leader of Datars. They are running among the thicket of warriors, deflecting one attack after another as Eld notices Tarat hidden behind a group of warriors slowly receding into the depths. But in vain, Eld and his warriors are already with them. They immediately cruelly reward themselves by killing one after another. Tarat is watching his army busy fighting from the safe distance and finds that he is left alone against a group of fighters. Then he raises his hands above his head and exclaims telepathically, "All right, you got me! We can make a deal now." Eld just laughs, and the others who follow him laugh as echo. "Do you really think, Tarat, that I want to make a deal with you now?" Tarat's eyes widen in fear, and he hisses with his thin tongue like a snake. "Stop it, Tarat, it won't help you." And then Eld thrusts a spear into him, pulls out his sword, and cuts off his head. While the body is slowly floating, the head remains in the Eld's hands. He lifts it over his head, there is blood everywhere. And he cries out to everyone: "Cease fighting! The battle is over now." He raises Tarat's head with one hand once more to prove that Datars have lost their leader. And their new leader is Eld Ion, the king of Ariads. Only now everyone stops and Datars surrender and humbly bow to all Ariads. "Now you will fight alongside me and my tribe of Ariads, and we will rule over this world together!" cries Eld, and everyone just nodds in agreement. Datars have no choice but to humbly agree because they have lost this battle.

However, deep in their hearts there will forever be just one leader and he is Tarat, the king of Datars.

They are going like greased lightning and being paralyzed with fear, Oliaf and others don't have time to look around. Hetchi, obviously in good mood, is calming Oliaf down with how he enjoys racing with the hybrids. However, they are not responding, they are pressing forward, like some machines. Even Aras doesn't react, all his thought focused only on one thing: to get home as quickly as possible. But it is still a very long way and there is no time to rest. They are passing the rocks, but something keeps nagging at Aras therefore he stops in front of the suspiciously looking rocks. All of them halt before the mountain they are about to cross. One of the fighters approaches him and asks telepathically: "What's the matter, brother?" Aras doesn't answer, he is just silently gazing into the distance. Oliaf also joins them and wonders carefully: "What's going on, brother?" Both the warrior and Oliaf look at each other, trying not to disturb Aras while he is observing the surroundings. He takes his time and finally turns to them and tells the warrior: "Look carefully into the distance, brother. What can you see in that mountain between two rocks?" and he points at the suspicious place. The warrior is doing his best but fails to see anything. "I can't see anything." Aras encourages him and points at the place again: "Look closer, brother, for it is very important. Our lives depend on that." The warrior is staring at the mountain, but he can't see anything. Finally, he asks: "What is it I shall see? What can you see there, brother?" Aras looks into the distance again, focusing on the space between the rocks and considering, because his guts are telling him something is not all right, but he can't explain it. "You know, brother, it might be nothing but when we were going this way before and when we were crossing that mountain, I had a strange feeling, as if we were being followed by someone. And now I might have seen something, but I can't describe what it is. I might be hallucinating, but I don't know." Frightened Oliaf intervenes in the conversation using his inner voice: "So what do you suggest? Because I haven't got wind of anything either." Aras looks at both of them, then at all the tired wanderers behind them, waiting impatiently for what he is going to say. "It is an extremely hard decision to make and there are not many options. Either we will cross that suspiciously looking mountain or we will get around it which will be safer but much more difficult because that journey will be long and exhausting and not that safe after all." Everybody is looking at Aras and expecting his decision. Aras is wavering, he has no idea what to do. He is running his fingers along the blade of his sword and thinking. Finally, he utters: „Damn it! Let's cross the mountain, but we really need to be very careful because something about that mountain doesn't add up." Aras gathers his courage and steps forward. The others are following him hesitantly.

Carefully and slowly, they are crossing the mountain looking in all directions, even the dolphins are swimming only in their own good time in the direction Aras has suggested as specially menacing. Oliaf looks frightened, leaning on Hetchi, who is also petrified. The warriors are looking at each other, spears ready in case something attacks them. They are going steadily up the rocky mountain, and the bubbles are bursting to the surface. They have already reached both rocks. They are advancing very slowly, expecting the worst, but in the end, everyone heaves a sign of relief. They have passed through the rocks and only the way home is awaiting them. They are almost blinded by the vision of their home so close when out of the blue a huge crocodile's mouth jumps out of nowhere and bites one of the warrior's head off. Aras immediately spots the whole gang of crocodiles resurfacing all around. In his mind he shouts to everybody to move on. He draws his sword, cuts one of the crocodile's head off, and immediately lunges forward. Oliaf, feeling completely numb, doesn't even react when one of the crocodiles is swimming up to him. Fortunately, he is rescued by a commanding warrior who stabs the crocodile with his spear from below. The two then end up in each other's arms, and then Oliaf sees it. He notices the face of a warrior and for a moment he is stunned. He doesn't quite understand what he has just seen. The commanding warrior is a pretty woman, looking like a fairy – warrior. A beautiful face, no hair though, and those gorgeous greenish eyes which are almost hypnotizing him as if the time has stopped for a while. Then he wakes up into the reality again and the female warrior is stabbing one crocodile after another and shouts in her mind: "Do you intend to keep staring at me forever now?!" Fortunately, Hetchi is here, taking Oliaf on his back and they are racing away, followed by the female warrior and the other warriors. Suddenly, however, the crocodiles pull down another guide. Oliaf shouts: "No, no, no, my brother!" And witnessing the death of his friend from the distance, he is almost in tears. Everyone is watching helplessly, the female warrior feeling sorry for crying Oliaf as they are dashing away from a gang of crocodiles. Aras is cutting his way forward with his sword, bouncing off one crocodile after another with the help of the warriors. In the end, they manage to escape. The crocodiles are pretty fast in the depths of the ocean, but obviously not fast enough. It's pointless for them to waste their energy, so they give up and they are just feeding on their prey. The horrified and mournful creatures are hurrying home, the huge mountain of Asads is within striking distance. They are approaching the walls, and their faces are grieving when Aras is sounding his trumpet to signal their comeback.

Asads and their king Ardax are already expecting them fervently.

All Ariads are having a rest in their dark fortress, and they are recovering their strength for a fight against another enemy. Eld is waking up from quite a weird dream, being hunted by a sort of nightmare, something he can't name. It is a recurring dream, possibly a message which he can't understand right now. This part of his consciousness hasn't developed well enough yet and he doesn't know how to use it. The others are also waking up, being watched by Eld. He is thinking about what's going on in his expanding kingdom, about the fate of all the creatures. Datars are locked in their cells and thoroughly supervised. Lapads are also isolated but they have already adapted and are obedient enough to be chained to the rocks and they can move a bit.

Uri begins to massage him gently from behind, and Eld relaxes, turns to his sweetheart and kisses her on the mouth. "I love you, my dear." Uri smiles tenderly. "I love you too, my love. I'm worried about you, and I'm always tormented by the idea that you won't come back." Eld looks at Uri and assures her that there are no reasons to be afraid and undoubtedly, they will be able to win the war for the rule over the world. "Uri, darling, believe me - and this is a personal guarantee - that we will win this war and live freely in great prosperity. I swear to my death." Uri grins, looks at her dear Eld with a shadow of a doubt in her eyes and answers: "Don't make any promises, honey. I believe in you; I will always believe in you. Just come home safe and sound each and every time, I will be waiting for you. My job is to protect our home together with my sisters but if you happen to need our help, we are ready to fight by your side, you know that." Eld smiles again and replies: "Just keep waiting for me here, my dear, and be prepared to defend our home. I will never let anything bad happen to you and you will never have to fight." "I know, love, I just want you to know I always have your back." Eld kisses her beloved Uri again, stands up, takes his armor and walks out of his tent. They are getting ready for another fight. While the others are still just waking up, Eld is fencing with the invisible enemies. After a while he shouts: "Get ready now! Another fight is about to begin!"

Chaos reigns throughout the kingdom as it is trying to fulfill Eld Ion's command. His son Lex is trying to speak to the king already lost in his thoughts. "What's happened, father?" he asks him with frightened thoughts. Eld breaks out of his thoughts and replies: "My son, don't ask me questions that aren't important at all. Does something always have to happen when I command a fight?" He looks angrily at his son. Lex looks fearfully into his father's eyes. Eld reads the fear in his eyes. "You see, my son, the warrior should always and under any circumstances be ready to fight. After all, we can only defeat our opponent if he doesn't expect it. The moment of surprise sometimes plays a big role, just as I see it in your eyes. You still have a lot to learn, but don't worry, my son, one day you will be a great warrior and ruler, and you will rule an empire in which you will no longer have to fear anything." Lex calms down a bit after Eld's words and goes after his shark to they could go on another fight with their friend Et. He understands that any more words will be pointless, so he will rather act so as not to disappoint his father.

The entire kingdom is up and about, the army is gathering and ranking into one combat formation. Lapads loaded with the rocks are led by the whole army of the warriors. Datars are now unwilling allies, completely helpless. They will simply have to fight by Eld Ion's side. Eld swims around his entire army on his shark to inspect it properly. Then he addresses them telepathically: "I can see some creatures which have doubts about me as a king, but it doesn't matter. You will understand why we are here. Now you will see I was right. Even the greatest doubters in this struggle will cease to doubt. Even the greatest unbelievers will begin to believe that you are fighting on the right side, because I am only interested in the welfare of you all. That's why I'm asking you to follow me," Eld Ion says and sets off ahead. The whole army, like a moving snake, sets out after him. There are a lot of fighters, no one will want to stand up to them anymore. Or? Would anyone be brave enough to stand up to such a cruel and numerous army? It would hardly occur to any creature that there was a kingdom that could threaten Eld Ion and his empire. But such a kingdom is yet to be found. It is a tribe of Madrians. They are very numerous, and their king Fagorus is very cruel, and Eld himself has great respect for him. That's why he's so focused on this fight. These are not just any weak fighters. They are predatory creatures with big, pointed teeth and red snake-like eyes. They can terrify the shit out of everyone. Their reddish skin with black spots all over their bodies makes them not easy opponents. He has been losing his sleep over this fight that's why he has decided to gather his army as quickly as possible and attack them. Madrians' heads are covered with wrinkled scales from the top and look disgusting. They are rumored to be fast and brutal warriors, but in the key battle they failed and betrayed Eld. They hunt in big groups, and they are brave enough to attack even stronger creatures that could threaten the life of any warrior in this kingdom.

The army is marching on the bottom of the ocean in this paradise world, sensing the great battle that will decide about the future of this world. Madrians are already waiting hidden in the depths, hidden in the different cracks, lurking for that big army. Eld and his army stop after a long journey. This has already become his ritual. He always stops and listens to his instincts and feelings that always reveal his enemy's weaknesses to him. He takes his time and keeps watching the depths and after some time the addresses Madrians telepathically: „Madrians! Madrians! Madrians! I am asking you, Fagorus, to surrender. We don't have to fight; we can just make a deal...“ He is waiting for a reply. Nothing. Even the sand on the bottom remains motionless. Eld is staring into the distance and thinking. His son Lex and the army's commander Tad approach him. Tad asks: "Well, what now, my lord? Are we going to keep moving forward or are we just going to keep staring into the emptiness, where there is nothing, not even the tiniest creature?“ Eld is just watching, ignoring Tad. When Lex's patience runs out too, he comes even closer to his father and asks in his thoughts: „Come on, father, what can you see? Tell us. We have no idea what we are waiting for.“ However, Eld just keeps staring into the distance. After what seems to have been ages, he turns to his son and looks deep in his eyes. Suddenly his thoughts begin to speak to everyone: "Are you ready to fight?“ They all answer unanimously: "Of course we are!“ "Well, it's about time we drove these cowards out of their shelters!“ Since everyone is waiting eagerly, he orders: "Attack!“ and he dashed forward into the strange depths of the ocean. Everybody is following him, in an attempt to overtake. They are sweeping forward like a tidal wave, leaving the dust behind them so thick that not even horses would be ashamed of. Suddenly those malicious creatures emerge from their cracks and attack them. The limbs are flying all around, blood is obscuring everything so nobody can see their hands, but Ariads are skilled warriors, and their blows are falling thick and fast. Eld catches the sight of Fagorus who is leading his army and immediately runs after him together with his fellow warriors. They are fending off one attack after another and then Fagorus notices him in the moment, which is not right for Eld, and he also heads forward accompanied by his group which is supposed to protect him. They come close and jump at each other. Everything freezes in that moment; the warriors stop fighting and they are watching Fagorus. He freezes for an instant too and suddenly his body is cut in half. Eld has done that to him. Fagorus doesn't gets a chance to retaliate, and the death is already carrying him into another world. He takes one last breath and smiles without uttering a word. The two halves of his body are floating in the space. Eld raises his sword above his head and yells telepathically: "You are all mine now, Madrians, you are my warriors, mine and no one else's. You are going to give in and fight by my side!"

Madrians kneel and pay homage to Eld, the king of Ariads.

22

Ardax and Aras are hugging each other so tightly they can't even breathe, but they don't care. They haven't seen each other for so long and they can't break away from each other. "My friend, please tell me you are bringing the good news," begs Ardax. However, Aras is unable to think clearly after what had happened to them before they reached the fortress of Asads. He looks at Ardax with his sad grieving eyes. "Ardax, my dear friend, I am struggling to find the right words. I wasn't able to protect everybody, and it is all my fault." "Aras, I can't help you to deal with it now. I can feel your sorrow, but we need to stay strong because we have found out that Ariads managed to defeat the strategic enemies and the predators are beginning to mobilize." Oliaf, in an embrace with everyone present, joins Ardax and Aras. "Please forgive me, I have been listening to your conversation. I think we are able to defeat the predators." They both look at each other and Ardax asks: „What do you mean? How can we defeat our enemy?" Oliaf is excited, and he is about to say something when a female voice starts speaking in their minds.

"He believes that if we can mobilize without a fight and unite all the peaceful creatures with the help of the guards, in an amicable way, the way of love, our chances are far from slim." Ardax and Aras look at a pretty warrior who has just put her warrior mask down. She has a lovely figure with the skin in a shape of braid on her head, a beautiful young face and blue and greenish complexion. Oliaf is speechless. He is staring at the gorgeous female warrior. After a long moment Ardax asks: "And who are you, lovely, strange lady?" The female warrior just smiles at all those dumb faces and introduces herself: "I am Ilemis, princess from the kingdom of the guards and daughter of Eliah, the king of our empire." Everybody is stunned. It turns out that her companions, those warriors who are accompanying Aras and Oliaf, are actually women. Incredibly beautiful women and suddenly all the women from the kingdom of Asads envy them. Ardax stops that excitement from the female warriors after a long time and asks: „Ilemis, daughter of my brother Eliah, what are you suggesting?" Ilemis looks at the entire kingdom in a surprise. "It isn't so bad with you; you just need a proper training and a strong discipline. I couldn't help noticing that you lack the discipline. You can't keep the strategical formations and that's why you will fail in the fight against the lord of the predators. Therefore, we have come here. Our mission is to prepare you for this great war." They are silently considering Ilemis's words until Ardax intervenes again: "Let us begin then." Ilemis and her fellow female warriors are extremely exhausted. "But we could also get some rest first, no?" she looks at Ardax pleadingly. He just smiles and this time he hugs Ilemis. "Well, of course. Please forgive us, but we are so desperate that we have forgotten our tradition of welcoming our guests warmly. I am very glad that my brother's daughter has honored us with her visit." Ardax lets go of Ilemis and orders Assads to prepare the visitors a place for rest. Ilemis and her comrades-in-arms go to see Ardax, and after a while, when Aras nods, he shows them their homes.

Ilemis and her comrades-in-arms thank them and go to rest in a small guest's dome.

23

Our mind is always full of our thoughts. We can't stop thinking. Once we have done something, we start thinking about our next step. Thoughts are our future and our past. We are thinking about what will happen if we do something. For example, when we have a dream at night. A dream often affects our thoughts, and we don't know what it means. And when our dream comes true, it pushes us further towards other dreams and plans. Each creature is driven by their dreams and Ariads aren't an exception. Dreams will never stop. Ariads' dreams always come true, and it pushes their thoughts closer and closer to their needs. Their needs are moving their dreams further and further into the depths of time they don't know.

There is a great party going on. Ariads are celebrating their victory over Madrians, but Eld knows very well they have come just halfway. Silent music is playing on the silent musical instruments, everyone is dancing and having fun. Lex is interested in one lovely girl that Et showed to him. He is trying to gather his courage to approach this girl with two scaly braids on her head, black and red skin, and a beautiful symmetrical face. She looks back at Lex and just at that moment Eld pats his shoulder: "Just go, son, you deserve that most wonderful love ever. Just go, son, and don't worry, she feels the same about you," he encourages him and winks also at Et who has also picked one gorgeous girl. Lex is gazing at his awesome girl, and she is smiling, letting him know she is attracted to him. Finally, he takes the plunge and comes to her. The girl is waiting for her dear Lex whom she picked a long time ago, but the right time to be introduced to each other has come just now. Lex approaches her, anxious and having butterflies in his stomach. He has no idea what to say to her. Finally, he decides to end this embarrassing moment and he utters: "Hello, my name is Lex." The girl smiles and replies: "I know who you are, but you are so sweet. I am Era Vilja." Lex smiles back at her, takes her hand, pulls her closer to him and kisses her cheek. She kisses him back. "Shall we go for a walk, or would you like to dance with me?" Era Vilja keeps smiling and says: "You know what? Let's dance first and then we might go for a walk." "Sounds great." They are dancing together with the crowd which is monolithic and moving like a snake. The silent musicians playing different tunes are also dancing and the music they are creating is entertaining for everybody.

Eld and Uri are having a lovely time too. They are watching their strengthening kingdom, but Eld knows very well that his goal – the rule over the world – is still far away. He needs to conquer three huge kingdoms to take control over the empire of predators and then he will be facing a tough task: to conquer the empire of celestial creatures. The empire of the merciful doesn't cause him any worries, it will be fast although not easy process, because he has heard about the very strong empires of celestial creatures. He will beat them in the end. He is afraid of the empire of guards; they will be a tough nut to crack for him. They will cost him a lot and it will be an awfully long process. Eld is lost in his thoughts and at the same time his consciousness is returning into the present where all his kingdom is celebrating. Uri strokes his head and kisses his cheek. "You've been somewhere else again. Don't worry, everything will be fine. You know I am always by your side, and I will protect you and our son with my own life. I love you," says Uri to calm Eld down. He kisses her cheek. "I know you will but look at our son. He has already found his first love and I am worried it will take him off his path we have been paving for him." Uri looks into Eld's eyes. "Don't worry, my dear. Our son is very mature. He knows what he is doing, we just need to have faith in him. We can't ruin this for him." Eld grins at Uri and kisses her. "You are right. Everything is just the way it is supposed to be. Let's have some fun ourselves. We haven't been playing together for a very long time." Eld lifts Uri into his arms, and they swim away to a place where nobody will disturb them.

The celebration is calming down and everyone is lying down to get some sleep. Lex and Era are walking slowly and quietly, undisturbed and holding hands as if there were only the two of them in the world. They are enjoying each other's company. "Did you have a good time with me?" Lex breaks the silence to ease the small tension between them, which is still present, even after a nice dance. Era smiles kindly at Lex and tries to make it easier for him. "I felt incredibly good with you. You're truly kind." "I'm glad. Will you come with me? I want to show you something." Era looks a little surprised. "Of course. And what is it you want to show me?" Lex just smiles darkly and grabs Era's hand. He starts swimming, Era joins him. They are swimming high, past everything. Lapads, the enemies defeated by Ariads, are glaring at them bluntly, but the two are just racing about. They are both screaming with joy in their minds, and their joy resounds throughout the realm. They reach the top of the hill that surrounds the whole empire. It's very big and they look around from its peak. Era perceives all the beauty lit up by the vast bottom of the ocean, which is their whole world and to which they belong, with silent amazement. "It's beautiful. So, is this what you wanted to show me?" Era asks in an astonished tone of thought. Waiting for what will come next, she looks lovingly into Lex's eyes. He looks right back at her and kisses her on the mouth. It is a lingering passionate kiss, they are burning with passion, they take off their clothes and start making love. Their bodies are melting into one, the whole world around them suddenly disappears, there are just the two of them in their own world, belonging just to them. A fire that they have never known before awakens in them and it now fills their hearts. Everything is revolving around them, and they are revolving around everything. Love unites the evil that it itself does not know, and the evil does not know love. They don't know what it is, but it subconsciously connects them, because when they need an offspring, they have to accept it. The climax comes after the passionate lovemaking of both love-connected creatures to beget their kid. And the dark dreamworld does not know that it will eventually be ruled by love and mercy. The lord of darkness has no idea that he is beginning to lose this war, because his dream of a material infinite paradise cannot be fulfilled without love. He is now anchored in the material world, and he cannot prevent love from controlling some merciful souls and restore their memory, to get them into the material world.

The two predators in love have just finished, they are getting dressed, enjoying what has just sparkled between them. They smile at each other and look each other in the eye with love, kissing again to confirm their relationship. Then, for a moment, they are watching the entire lighted realm, full of the creatures going to bed. They both walk back to this expanding realm in silence, for now they do not need any words for what has arisen between them. They kiss passionately again. "I'm so happy. I love you, Era, my dear." He kisses her passionately again. "I love you very much too, my dear Lex. But it's time to get back to our families." Lex nods, confirming Era's thought. "I love you." "And I love you." They both confirm it again. They find it difficult to break away

from each other and can't think of anything but their love. Lex returns to
the place where he will go to his room in their small palace to have
a rest.

Eld is secretly looking at his son and thinking. But he, too, returns to the
room to Uri, who is already asleep and immersed deep in the dream
world.

24.

It is a wonderful dream, to live in the never-ending paradise in unlimited love where everyone respects and loves each other. It is a wonderful dream in which Ilemis, princess of the realm of the guards, finds herself now. She adores everything that is alive, but it keeps vanishing into thin air right in front of her and everyone is dying. She can see it clearly. She grabs her spear and throws it into the unknown space and hits Eld Ion, the king of Ariads, who is still bringing the disaster upon them. He is destroying everything around; everyone is bleeding, and the suffering doesn't seem to end any time soon. Ilemis bursts into tears, she can see that killing Eld Ion was pointless. A new war is about to begin, the war whose ending remains a mystery to all of them. Ilemis is weeping, asking for forgiveness when suddenly... she is waking up in Oliaf's arms and he is smiling at her. "Don't worry, dear princess, it was just a nightmare." Ilemis jumps up and reprimands Oliaf, asking him how he dared come in. Oliaf just raises his hands and defends himself from the attacks of angry Ilemis. "What are you doing here?!" she keeps yelling in her thoughts and other female warriors also stand up, draw out their spears and aim them at him. „I am deeply sorry, ladies, I meant no harm. I just saw dear Ilemis have a bad dream. I have studied the thoughts that accompany us while we are sleeping since forever and I still don't know what they mean." "So you decided to spy on us without our prior agreement? That's not something polite creatures will do!" says Ilemis furiously and other female warriors nod. "Please forgive me, I was attracted here because I had never come across such a crystal-clear thought as Ilemis had before," Oliaf is trying to explain his motif. Suddenly Ardax enters and asks surprisingly: "What's going on here?" Everyone turns to Ardax and Ilemis says: "This creature of yours is bothering us with his nonsense." "Really? What nonsense?" Ardax looks at Oliaf indignantly. He raises his hands again as if to protect himself from something and replies: "I never wanted to bother anyone. You know me, my lord, I would never harm a soul. But it came to me again, I saw those thoughts during the sleep." "You saw that again? However, it isn't an excuse for bothering our guests during their sleep." "Yes, yes, you are absolutely right, my lord, but I couldn't help myself. Once I notice it, I have to look deeper."

Ardax understands Oliaf very well because recently he has also been interested in dreams. Those dreams which these creatures don't understand yet, they are unable to explain what they are. Oliaf is the one who is trying to get at the root of it. Ardax turns to the ladies. "Please, forgive our friend for interrupting your nap, but I have to speak in his favour. He has been trying to figure out what illusions are running in our heads when we are sleeping. Nobody can explain what it means." The female warriors are silent for a moment and then their wave their hands and smile: "All right, we can't explain that either and we have never thought about it in this way, and we had no idea somebody is dealing with it. However, it still isn't an excuse for his behavior." "I get it and I assure you it won't happen again, not without your consent. Right, Oliaf, my friend?" Ardax is speaking in a very firm voice and Oliaf just nods. "It will never happen again; you have my word. I am begging for your forgiveness." He bows to all the ladies, and he is leaving. "My friend is really obsessed with what's happening to us while we are sleeping." "Now when you are speaking about it, I also find it quite interesting. We have never thought about it before." "Oliaf is an expert in this, he has already managed to explain one of the ideas that came out of it, but then he came across some inconsistencies again." "What inconsistencies?" "You have to talk to Oliaf about it, because only he can explain this issue more precisely." "I'm very interested, so I'll ask him about it." "Anyway, he's a very nice guy, but also pretty vulnerable." "I noticed that. I wouldn't even believe that he's been on so many journeys around this world when he can't even defend himself. It's incredible." "You're right, Princess Ilemis, but he's so resourceful that he can escape from any threat." "Well, I don't quite agree. I'd say he has good luck." "Oh, come on, there is more to it. He has an astonishing ability to anticipate danger." "Nonetheless, I think he's a fool. We have to train him in combat, because only then will he be a very good fighter with such abilities." "You're right, now we have a great opportunity to train him in combat." "Yes, you are also right, Ardax, brother of my father and the king of Asads. I have heard a lot of rumors about you from my father Eliah and I feel a great respect to you. I will do my best to help you fight against the predators." Ardax stretches all his joints and says: "Well, it's time to start training!" And he steps out of the guest's dome. The female warriors get up, also stretch all their joints, and go out, following their princess.

Outside, everyone is doing their thing and the female warriors with the princess are just watching the whole area. "I know, I know, you don't have to tell me anything. These will be our allies. Our task will be to gather them in large numbers. As I see it, in exceptionally large numbers." And suddenly a group of strange smiling young Assads approaches. "Oh, bloody hell, I already feel like an attraction that entertains the others," states princess's best friend Rejasis. The whole group surrounds them when suddenly Aras appears out of nowhere. "That should be enough. Leave our guests alone! Get out of here!" The group scatters here and there as Aras disperses them. "We haven't even thanked you yet." "What do you want to thank me for?" "Well, for helping us get here." "Oh, don't mention it." "We truly appreciate it. Thank you very much." "You are welcome. I'm here to escort you to the training ground. It is about time we started training, because we will have to set out on a journey to unite the other kingdoms that will fight for us." "So, there will be more?" "Hm, so much more. There are a lot of various peaceful kingdoms worth noticing when it comes to fight." "Aras, there is something I'd like to ask you. Where did you learn to fight so well? You don't seem to be one of them." Aras smiles and answers: "It's a long story which I will tell you about when the time is right."

They arrive in a large area where a huge group of Assads determined to fight is already waiting. Oliaf is also among them, overly excited and he is looking at Ilemis with a smile. She just smirks and looks away from Oliaf, as if to show him her pride. Ardax speaks to everyone. "I don't have to introduce these ladies to you. They are very experienced fighters who have come to help us, so I ask you to obey them in everything. Do you all understand that?" The whole crowd says in unison: "Yes!" "Well, everything is ready, you can start training now." Ilemis looks at the determined group. "I have to admit, this doesn't look so bad anymore. You will be an army that will fight for all peaceful creatures against the cruel warriors, the predators. You have to keep it in your mind and listen to me carefully. At first, let me give you one good and crucial piece of advice. It concerns fear. Fear is your greatest enemy, but it might become your friend as well. You must learn to control it. You must get rid of it while you are fighting, stop thinking about it and focus only on the fight itself. But before the fight, fear is good as it sharpens your senses so you can identify the strength of your enemy and reveal his weaknesses." Everyone is thinking about Ilemis's advice. Ardax and Aras are just smiling, and they are starting to like this training. Ilemis continues: "Now everyone will take their makeshift weapons, we will try the attacks. Make pairs and stand against each other. Attack as you would!" She says: "Attack!" All the pairs begin to attack each other quite awkwardly. The female warriors are all looking at each other and rolling their eyes. "So, this will cost us a great deal of patience and it will be hard and challenging work. Keep going! Get into it! Again, and again! Attack! Defense!" Ilemis is shouting in her thoughts. She is already losing her patience. The merciful are doing their best and the female warriors are helping them in the meantime, adjusting their attack and defense techniques. Everyone is watching the female warriors intently.

And they are learning to fight against their fear as well. The fear that they are going to hurt someone but also the fear for their life.

25

Morning lovemaking is a wonderful way how to start a new day. Two young souls are making love and there is just their private world, nothing else is real. Love connects them again; they have forgotten about the war raging around them all their lives. The war for the world domination, started by Eld Ion. Lex has just reached the climax of love of two young souls and Era is gently cuddling him. All of a sudden, they can hear the sound in their minds announcing the gathering of the warriors in the typical place. Another battle is coming, and it is supposed to enlarge the group of Ariad soldiers. Eld is calling everyone, and the entire army is waking up to get ready for another journey at the end of which they will fight against Neorids.

Neorids are led by a very reasonable king who would also love to take control over this world. They have already won a few battles and they have become a very annoying competitor in this battle for the world domination. Neorids are specific also because of their yellow and greenish skin. Their heads are almost crocodile-like, but their mouths are smaller, and their bodies are the same as the bodies of other already developed creatures with high intelligence and great creativity and adaptability to their environment. They are highly organized and loyal to their king Kalder. Kalder is quite robust and very muscular; he has a small mouth and scaly stripes on the head. Not only he is a big and dreaded killer, but he is also highly intelligent, a perfect strategist and speaker and all Neorids respect him. Their small realm is dangerous for Eld, but Ariads are already so powerful that they can afford to attack Neorids who also abandoned Eld in the battle against the celestial creatures. Just as Eld, also Kalder has one great weakness – his family and wife Defen. Eld knows he needs to protect his own family and watch out for the family of the king Kalder. Neorids live in an exceptionally large fortification full of huge rocks. They are very well equipped with deadly weapons, so Eld is even more concerned before this battle. Well, and besides, there are two other very powerful kingdoms that he needs to get to his side in order to gain dominance over the world of predators and finally be able to march against the celestial creatures.

Now they are all lined up, feeling fresh and strong, prepared for another battle. Eld looks at his son, who is saying goodbye to Era Vilja and then joins his father. Et follows Lex as if he was his shadow. Eld looks maliciously in Lex's eyes and shakes his head. "Lex, Lex, Lex, you will never learn, but never mind, it's good. Even love can rouse us for action. You just have to realize that you will bear the consequences and it will hurt a lot when you have to decide between love and being a king." "I don't know what you're talking about, father, but I hope I will get it one day." Still shaking his head, Eld smirks and turns to his entire very large army, ready to set out on a long journey to the higher place where the Neorid fortress resides. "I hope you all rested well, and your wounds are healed, because now we have a very big battle ahead of us. Are you all ready to fight for our kingdom?!" Everybody replies: "Yes, we are ready!" "Let's go then!" He shouts into the minds of his army again, and it moves like one huge boa out of their fortified empire, leaving just a cloud of dust behind them. The cloud so thick it is almost impossible to see the whole army hidden in the huge swirling cloud of dust. Not even to see the whole rolling army, but just a huge swirling cloud of dust. Everything is rumbling and roaring, the ground at the bottom of the ocean is shaking.

Neorids can hear the noise and feel the ground under their feet quaking. The commander of their army and the chief advisor to King Kalder Féder asks with fear in his throat: "Is that them, my lord?" "Yes. Call the militia at once." Féder, even mightier than his master, with huge and sharp teeth and rougher scales on his head, just blows his horn loudly. Everybody begins moving immediately, they are preparing for a big battle. "There are so many of them," says Féder, and Kalder just looks silently into the distance, where he can feel the roar of the incoming Ariad army. "Prepare shields to strengthen the fortress!" Feder passes the command on to the peaceful creatures, who are doing hard work here. Neorids also have their own methods how to treat the peaceful creatures. They enslave them, use them and finally they eat them. Kalder keeps staring into the distance, feeling that roar and rumble more and more. He knows they have a little advantage as they are a bit higher and huge place near the surface of the ocean, and they can even see a bit of the starlight coming down to this beautiful planet. They call this uncharted territory the heavens. Now Kalder can already see that big army of Ariads, coming straight at them and leaving them speechless. They have never seen such an army and they are frightened and anxious. "That fool has succeeded, but we won't give up," shouts the king to calm his warriors down. The army of Ariads surrounds Neorids standing on that higher place in the local rocks on the top of the sub-oceanic mountain. However, this is not a drawback for Ariads, it is easy to swim up to the surface and attack Neorids. Neorids are well armed though, so the attack from the top might not be that simple.

Eld stops the army, orders them to hold their positions. As usual, he looks into the distance to assess the situation. He is looking for weaknesses in the Neorid fortress. He has already chosen a strategy, but his tradition is to try it in a peaceful way, as he does it before every battle. He challenges Neorids to surrender to him. Kalder just starts to laugh and his whole army follows his example. Eld is laughing, but this time together with them, and Kalder finds it confusing. "You know very well that you have no chance. That is why I am giving you a unique opportunity to join me, and you will earn my respect." Kalder laughs again. "I like that, but you know that I can't put my pride in my pocket." "Forget about your pride, it won't save you from the defeat." "I guess our negotiation is over. Don't you think Eld Ion, king of Ariads?" "Well, I wanted to give you a chance to save your fortress. I will get you, Kalder, king of Neorids!" Eld waits a bit longer before he orders his army to attack. The first shots are ready, but they will be just stray to scare the enemy psychologically. Then he is planning to send a small group of the warriors to the top to fire some shots towards the inside of the fortress. But Eld is still waiting for Kalder and his army to suffocate in their fear. After a while, he issues an order in his mind: "Shoot up there!" He points upwards, and the underwater cannons, which are supplied with huge, elongated stone prisms topped by sharp points, fire precisely. Stunned Calder and Neorids set up their shields, as the impact of the prisms throws many fragments of huge rocks towards them. Eld then gestures with his hand to a small group of infantries to attack the fortress from above. This small group embarks on a suicidal attack and is immediately under heavy fire of various oblong stone shots. But they can complete the task and fire small, elongated bullets from their firearms towards the fortress. A few defenders fall from the fortress wall, but Neorids respond immediately and the whole small group is crushed soon. Eld just smiles, immediately orders another attack from all sides, but this time to the bottom of the fortress. Everyone is amazed at this order, but

Eld knows very well what he is doing. He frowns at his warriors and, with great anger, repeats the order in his mind. "Fire, damn it!" Everyone immediately comes to their senses and shoots from all sides at the bottom of the fortress. Elongated stone stakes are flying, the fortress and the whole mountain is trembling in the foundations. Kalder and all Neorids are frightened and Féder asks: "What do you think? Will it last?" "Start shooting at all positions!" "But it will be pointless." "It doesn't matter, our families have to run away." "But they can't. There is no way out." "I was thinking about this situation. They have to run away." "Okay but look around. Even if you use the escape route, Ariads are everywhere, and you know very well what will happen on a large area when they see them flee." "Of course, I do know that. So, wait a moment, but shoot at all positions." "Everyone, get ready and shoot!" Kalder is thinking. The fortress is still shaking, and it is a just a matter of seconds until the whole mountain and the fortress fall. Féder only orders everyone to shoot at positions, but they will only be warning shots to interrupt for a moment the thunder that is shaking the entire fortress. Eld is smiling while the others don't understand. Lex walks over to his father. "What on earth are they doing? I don't get it. Don't they know we are at the safe distance and their shots can't reach us?" Eld looks at Lex seriously and shakes his head. "Lex, Lex, Lex, there are still so many things you need to learn. Never underestimate your enemy. They know very well that their shots can't reach us but look around. Their purpose isn't to hit us, but to create the chaos they need to be able to maneuver or escape." "Really? But they will never succeed!" "I know that without you, my stupid son. Listen to me now and watch me, because now is the right time you learnt something." Eld waves his hand at the group that is protecting him and together with Lex and Et, riding their sharks, they come closer to the fort. They are circling around and Eld suddenly shouts in his mind: "Oh, just look at them! Do you see that little group?" He points in the distance. Everyone is just watching with their mouths open, trying to understand what's going on in that distance. "That's exactly what I was expecting from those cowards. Go after them!" Eld says. They move forward on their bloodthirsty sharks, but Eld is pouring oil on troubled waters. Kalder turns back and sees the small group chasing them. He understands, halts his gang that is startled and looking at him. "Stop. Running away is pointless, they will catch us. There is just one solution." Kalder's Gader and the desperate others say promptly: "No, we need to run!" "No, it will be in vain. They are with us any minute soon and you know what that means. There is no point in running away. I have to challenge Eld to a duel, it's our only hope." "You can't do that. You will die." "I know and if there was another option, I'd go for it. But there isn't." Eld and his warriors are approaching, Kalder is standing still in his combat position, and he is waiting. As soon as Eld is just a few meters away, he issues an order: "Stop!" Everybody is waiting patiently. Eld is looking Kalder in his eyes and smiling. "Do you know what this means, Kalder, king of Neorids?" "I don't need to guess, I know what I have to do. It will be an honor to fight against you in a duel and I hope I will be a good opponent to you, and I will beat you." Eld starts laughing loudly so that everyone can hear it in their mind. Suddenly he yells at everyone to stop attacking. The entire army ceases to fight, and they are waiting. "I accept. At last, you will have a chance to prove you are not such a coward."

Kalder looks back, looking into the sad eyes of his family and his entire group. And he turns to Eld and his Ariads again.

26

A creature determined to fight after long training battles, in which he was accompanied by beautiful and tender creatures of guards, is fencing. His strikes at the virtual enemy he is imagining are precise. "I see that someone has improved their skills," the words of the beautiful trainer Ilemis interrupt him. Oliaf stops immediately, embarrassed, looking into the eyes of the gorgeous princess. "As I see it, you aren't completely hopeless." Oliaf grins and just looks humbly at the beauty that evokes his respect and awe. He can't find the words for what he wants to say to her. "Did you become tongue-tied during that training?" Feeling even more embarrassed, Oliaf looks into the ground and responds carefully: "I don't know what to say, my lady." "Well, well, now you are at a loss for words, but you are brave enough to disturb my sleep." "I, I, ..., I.." "Hush!", she puts her finger on his lips. "You have certain abilities that I find very interesting, and they might be the crucial element in this war. I'm not sure whether you understand how precious this gift of yours is, so don't ruin it. It's good that you are learning to fight but you should also work on that ability you obviously have." "What ability are you talking about?", asks confused Oliaf. "Good lord, you really don't know, do you? Even better. You are able to find a key, but you don't know how to use it." "What key?" "Good grief, and you are also stupid. I was speaking metaphorically, silly." She runs her finger along his cheek gently, but Oliaf is just staring at her, having no idea what this is about. "I will have to pay special attention to you, my darling, I guess. I think my father will like you too. Even though you already know each other, he thinks you are a nitwit who came scared to death to pass on a message. But at that time, he didn't know yet - none of us did - that you have the gift we need in this war." "I don't understand what you are saying, but I hope there is an explanation." "An explanation? You already have one right in front of your eyes, you just can't see it yet. So, now start defending yourself, I'm going to test your combat skills, and maybe you'll also discover your special ability, you little fool." She immediately draws a makeshift spear and attacks Oliaf straight away. Before he is able to do anything, she hits him in his head and knocks him down. In a second, he is lying on the ground and Ilemis is grabbing him by the scruff of his neck. Oliaf is fidgeting in a surprise. "See how stupid you are? You still don't get it. But don't worry, I'll teach you how to understand things." "I have no idea what it is you want from me." "Now I want you to defend yourself." "All right, I will." Ilemis laughs out loud, attacks Oliaf once more, but this time he avoids her very deftly and he tries to cut her with his makeshift sword. Suddenly they are interrupted by a strange voice of thought: "Stop, stop, please." Ilemis almost fails to hide her disappointment, but she notices Ardax, the revered king of this realm, so she is especially kind to him and greets him with a slight bow. "Greetings, my lord. As you can see, we're just practicing the art of fighting here with your friend." "I am sorry for disturbing you in such an important training, but I'd like you to go with me now, Ilemis, I need to have a quiet word with you, if you know what I mean." Ilemis smiles a bit, rubs gently at Oliaf who pulls away in embarrassment. "Hm, I can see that your friend is pretty shy." Ardax smiles back at her. "Just give him some time. There are a lot of things he still doesn't understand, although he has been through a lot already, through more than you and me." "I am aware of that. So, what it is that you want to tell me, my lord?" "Dear Ilemis, my princess, it's about time we set out on another journey as soon as possible. Our very good friends have just returned from the nearby corners of our world, and they have witnessed something terrible." Ilemis is lost in her thoughts and then she asks: "And who are these friends of yours and what exactly did they see?"

Ardax leads the princess to a small group of the blueish creatures with small beaks and slight yellowish lines decorating their blue skin. They are a bit slim and short, but very quick. Whoever meets these well-trained creatures, has every right to be scared. Their eyes are oval, a little funny, which amuses Ilemis. "What can you tell me about yourselves, you ridiculous creatures?" The creatures frown a bit, their small trunks on the sides of their heads that were supposed to be ears, pull back. "We beg your pardon, lady, but we are Etorets and we also belong to - as you call it - the celestial world." "Well, and have you ever met any predators?" The small group of Etorets just smiles mildly and one of them, most likely their leader, approaches Ilemis so fast that she doesn't have any time to get ready for a fight. "Easy, we are peaceful creatures, and we wouldn't be able to kill somebody just like that. I am Flitur, the king of Etorets." Flitur takes a bow to show his respect to Ilemis and she does the same. "I am Ilemis, the princess of the guards that live exactly in the middle of everything that is going on in this world." "Very nice to meet you." "What brings you here?" Flitur looks Ilemis into the eyes, feeling scared. "Something horrible has happened. A bit further afield there live dangerous predators, Neorids, who have never heard about us since we live in the parts of the world completely unknown to others. Furthermore, we are fast, we can vanish into thin air in a second and move so quickly that they won't even notice. But something worrying has happened. We don't mind Neorids that much. However, those who attacked them obviously do. They even didn't give them a chance to defend themselves against such a superior army and weapons that are extremely terrifying and destructive." Ilemis takes a deep breath and immediately calls out: "In that case we'd better get going." Ardax summons the entire kingdom. "Get ready, we are leaving. The time has come, and we are going to set out on a journey together with our celestial brothers and sisters and join our forces to fight against a great evil that sees us just like their food." The creatures start moving and load everything necessary up. They know very well that their home won't be home anymore unless they stand against the realm of predators and help in the decisive battle for the world dominance. They all gather on one place, ready to depart. Ardax and Aras with their families are standing in front of the whole nation of Asads. Princess Ilemis and her female warriors are waiting in the back until Ardax starts his speech before they leave the fortress they have been protecting as their home for ages. Ardax is taking his time, just as the kings usually do it, to give their speech the proper emphasis. "Welcome. I have got two pieces of the news for you; one is bad, and one is good. I'll begin with the bad one. You know that we must leave this beautiful place. We have been building it up for so long. However, it's the high time we abandoned it. That's the bad news. The good news is that finally we have an opportunity to come out of our shell and fight for our freedom. Yes, I know you are worried about your life, but we must fight against the enemy who is keeping us trapped. We must break out and fight and this time win this battle for the world dominance and end these threats and danger we have been facing for ages. Trust me, if we win this war, we'll never have to be afraid again and we will live happily. I can guarantee that. That's the good news. Let's fight for our freedom, let's join our brothers and sisters. The other world needs to be united by war. We will be united by love, without any killings or wars and this will be our weapon. Let's do this!" orders Ardax, the king of Asads. The crowd is cheering, even Ilemis pays tribute to Ardax for his brilliant speech and when their eyes meet, she nods her head in respect.

Ardax gets on his dolphin and sets out on an adventure.

27

The crocodile creatures appear to be calm, but that's just an impression they are trying to make. They love pretending they are calm. As soon as the prey gets within their reach, they turn into extremely fast beasts. However, they have no chance against the sharks, therefore Kalder has agreed to meet Eld in the duel. Neorids are a sort of crocodiles too, that's why these have become their friends and serve them. Kaldor gets down from his means of transport and stands up against Eld. "Are you ready to fight, king of Neorids?" "Well, the question is whether you are ready to lose, Eld Ion, king of Ariads." Eld bursts out laughing, and everyone is waiting for the duel between the kings impatiently. Both are in a big circle on a vast area surrounded by the hedge made of living creatures. All of them are both judges and spectators, cheering their own king. "Let's fight to the finish." "Deal, the winner takes it all." The creatures can hear that in their minds, and they begin to roar. There are so many of them that it will be a great loot for the winner, especially for Kalder, because Eld has brought him an army that can fight against any enemies. Kalder has already understood that he can get the reign he has never even dreamt of. And now it is right here, on a silver platter. Is it fate? Eld is just smiling, he knows his enemy and the way this enemy leads the fight. Eld would never underestimate him, he knows he needs to be incredibly careful, but he also knows that if he is very patient, he can beat him at his own game.

This is a big challenge. The two of them get on their fellow warriors and means of transport in one. Eld is holding his long spear and there is a sword behind his back as a backup gun. Kalder is sitting on his crocodile, clutching his long spear too and his two swords are on his back. They are staring at each other, hypnotizing their opponent to distract him. The crowd is just watching silently, prepared for whatever may come. The makeshift arena is ready. Everybody knows that this duel might decide about who will rule the whole world. "Now we both will go away from each other to our edge of the circle and then we will return to each other, but that time it will be for real. Do you agree, Kalder, King of Neorids?" "Certainly. Let's do it!" They both set the boundaries for the beginning of a duel that basically has no rules. They head towards their makeshift living border. Eld is almost there, and he turns around and sees that Kalder's crocodile is a bit late. Kalder is not worried about whether he will be the first or second, what matters to him is the battle in which the crocodile is a bit defter and a particularly good helper in the fight. This is not only the fight between two kings, but also a fight between their creatures used as means of transport and helpers. That's why Eld waits a moment until Kalder gets to his place. It isn't a moral gesture at all, he does it to get a psychological advantage. Kalder has noticed this, and he is halting the impatient crocodile. The crocodile doesn't understand anything but listens to his master. Eld doesn't move an inch and it makes his shark angry. „Just hold on for a moment," Eld is keeping his shark calm to stop him from raging. Sharks are extremely aggressive and cagey creatures. They have seven senses. However, neither Ariads nor Neorids are far behind.

Kalder is watching what Eld is doing, and he is taking a little more time to get to his side, but he's already thought through the tactics, and he has almost got to his place. He turns around - and suddenly Eld isn't there. He looks up and sees him rushing at him at full speed on a furious shark. The crocodile moves a little forward, ready to attack. Eld is approaching like a jet, and when Kalder gets within range, he throws a spear in his direction. Kalder does not expect the spear not to be aimed at him but at the crocodile and it hits him in the head directly between the eyes. And so Eld first gets rid of the crocodile, which was his intention from the very beginning. The crocodile was a main threat and now it is gone. The crowd is shocked by what has just happened. The crocodile didn't have a chance to defend itself and now it is dead. Kalder has no time to cry over the loss of his long-term crocodile friend who served him so well. There is another raid coming from Eld. He immediately throws his spear at Eld's friend. He is expecting this move and yet hardly manages to avoid the attack and the spear scrapes the shark's face. Eld hits off the spear with his own sword and although he gets scraped by it as well, he saves his friend. The evasive maneuver is a success and Kalder is swimming towards the space upwards to have a better position to fight and especially to be in the space where he can better defend himself against the attacks of Eld and his shark. With a slight advantage, Eld again makes a quick raid on alerted Kalder. He fires at him at full speed, ready to finish him with his sword, but Kalder has two swords at his disposal, which makes him a rather dangerous opponent. He is a very experienced and good fighter who does not give up easily and is now even more dangerous because he has the motivation to avenge his friend. He deftly drives both swords and hits the shark again. Eld is also lurking there, using this moment and hitting Kalder in the back, but he immediately gathers his wits and returns the blow, but Eld immediately drives the injured shark away from danger, so Kalder's blow misses its target. Eld checks his friend for serious injuries, but he lets him know that he is fine and can continue in the next raid. Eld lingers for a moment, trying to figure out his enemy, wondering what maneuver he will choose now. He does not want to lose the advantage, because Kalder is extremely dangerous in the direct combat. He recalculates his movement and starts another thoughtful assault. Calder is waiting calmly, as if luring his enemy and focusing Kalder on him. Now he is using the instinct of a crocodile and waiting motionless in the space, as if he wasn't even breathing.

This nerve-wrecking duel is being watched by the tense crowd which is waiting for a winner. Eld is hurtling towards calm Kalder. His peace and quiet makes him anxious so he pulls the shark to the side to lead the attack not from above but from the side where he is more vulnerable. Kalder can foresee Eld's intention, he takes a defensive position and makes a move towards the shark. This time it isn't a smart act. Eld disappears from the sight for a while, jumps down from the shark in the last moment and cuts off Kalder's head. Everyone is struck dumb, not able to understand what they have just witnessed. Kalder's head and body are falling to the bottom. Eld is just smiling and halting the shark who is about to chase the prey and eat it up. He gets back on his shark and tries to keep him quiet. Then he comes closer to the dead crocodile and just to be sure it is dead; he cuts off his head too and pulls his spear out of it to raise it above his head as a sign of victory. He calls out in his mind: "Now you all belong to one huge realm! You are my warriors. You will fight by our side, led by me, against another of our enemies. Soon the entire world will belong to us and trust me, we will live in great welfare and peace. I promise you that!" Ariads are cheering and celebrating Eld, their king, the king of the great realm which needs to face just a few enemies in the depths of the ocean now. But they are also thinking about the celestial creatures who still pose a huge threat. Neorids are terribly disappointed, the queen and the whole family of the subjects are grieving over the lost king who will be long remembered. There is nothing they can do now because they are very vulnerable and they know that if they die, they can never avenge the king.

So, they choose to surrender to Ariads.

The giant wave is rolling near the surface of the strange ocean in the celestial world. There is a lovely light coming out of it and everyone admires it. The dolphins sometimes fly up above the border of the sea heavens and nobody can understand how they do it. Ardax, the strongest celestial king of Asads, also occasionally gets over the heavens and enjoys that mysterious beauty but he needs to get back quickly because he can feel the heat as his scaly skin is glittering. He is losing his strength and breath, and he is under the surface straight away.

The celestial beings are rushing to join their friends from the celestial kingdom of Cetefs. It is another royal realm that has emerged after the battle as one of the strongest, but they are too careful. The life of Cetefs is spiritual although they don't quite understand what it means but they are exploring, just like Oliaf, and trying to figure it out. Ilemis has also noticed this, and this idea is hunting her while they are rushing towards Cetefs. Ardax has just caught the sight of the high mountain behind the horizon, which is formed into a big tower on top of which those most extraordinary creatures of this world reside. "Careful, please, they have trust issues," says Oliaf. Everyone is alert and they slow down when they are within the reach of a gun. They approach the huge stone gate under the peak of the mountain. Suddenly there is the sound similar to the trumpet, but these are only the guards able to make the loud sounds similar to the sounds of the Asad entertainers when they are cheering up the warriors and showing them their support in the fight against the enemies. "Who are you and what are you doing here?" asks the whispering voice in the minds of the entire expedition. "Fear not, we are Asads, your friends, and our allies are here with us too." "These are very popular words these days." "I know, but I really mean it. We are coming in peace; you have my word. I am Ardax, the king of Asads." "Is that really you? It must be pretty serious when Ardax himself comes here together with such a big expedition armed to their teeth." Ardax is thinking for a moment. He understands that Cefets don't believe them. Therefore, he comes a bit closer so they can have a proper look at him. "It is truly you, Ardax, my friend," says elated mind voice. The gates open with screeching, a huge whirl of bubbles and big waves comes along and the whole expedition is literally trembling. As soon as the gates open, another wave of incredible noise reaches them, the noise that neither Ardax nor his expedition are used to. Neither Ardax himself nor Ilemis and her fellow female warriors understand this, they are only watching in astonishment how this whole kingdom could have developed in this way. It is now clear why Ardax needs Cetefs - they have nine more celestial armies scattered throughout the celestial world.

A celestial creature of light green, almost glittering green color, with yellow braids resembling the very thin hair on his head and with a broad smile is approaching the expedition with the open arms. His face is beautiful, even though the celestial creatures are almost toothless because their teeth which they don't need to use anymore, have just the visual effect. However, each creature – including the celestial one – might change into the heterotrophic being fast once they have tried any other living organism. But they do their best to avoid this, because their conviction and power is what keeps them alive for so long. Long life is possible only if you consume just water and absorb the energy of light. "Welcome, my dear friends. You have no idea how delighted I am to see you after such a long time, Ardax, brother." King Talaof is welcoming them dressed in the silver gown and he is hugging Ardax very tightly. "I am so delighted you are here. Please, follow me." Cetefs make a corridor. Some of them go on having fun – as if they were dancing samba – and they are telling each other some stories and the others are declaring their love to their partners. Each Cetef looks back and greets the guests respectfully with a slight bow. They are very tall, slender, and oblong, remarkably diverse in terms of clothing. Only skin color unites them all into one. They are very sociable, but also very mistrustful, you can see it in their faces. They don't like to reveal their thoughts to strangers, they hide them very quickly.

The whole expedition is heading to the centre of the kingdom where you can find the most influential beings in all the kingdom. They are swimming up to the gate which is in front of the one for the celestial creatures. Talaof makes a trumpeting sound to alert the guards and to ask them to open the gates to the honorable guests. The golden green gates are opening and revealing the magnificent glittering hall. Everyone is almost lit by the beauty they can see. A crowd of honorable beings is standing there. They are dressed in a kind of net gowns. The noble lords are welcoming this expedition with awe, but only the most important ones are allowed to enter the hall of kings. The others need to stay in front of the gates. Talaof gestures the noble of the expedition to follow him through the hall decorated with wonderful shimmering mosaics made up from tiny, one-centimeter big squares. They portray the famous celestial beings who meant something and left their trails in the history of this world. Ardax, Aras, Oliaf and Ilemis together with her six female guards are admiring this artistry. The noble ones are slowly making the corridor and they are whispering something to each other. Step by step they are getting closer and closer to the place where the most noble of all, nine kings, are already expecting and welcoming them with a deep bow and awe and a smile on their faces. Talaof comes to his throne. Each king has his own. But now it is time for the queen, who belongs to the main elements of this kingdom and whose word has the uppermost importance, to speak. Queen Ameris with nice braids on her head, the symmetrical face and the mouth typical for the celestial creatures, although small. "Welcome, Ardax, the king of Asads. What brings you here?" says queen Ameris. Her blue net gown is rippling in the water. Her slim figure makes her an adorable lady arousing respect of many kings and queens. "Greetings, queen Ameris. You are still as beautiful as you were when I last saw you. You know what brings me here, so I don't understand your question." Queen Ameris starts laughing, joined by others like an echo. Ardax looks at all those smiling kings and he is watching them with a serious expression on his face. Ilemis doesn't remain unresponsive either, but Ardax gestures to do nothing but listen. Everyone calms down after a while. "Well, Ardax, we all know what brings you here. But we aren't quite sure what you are expecting from us. It wasn't – or maybe it was – so long ago when you had a chance to get this throne, but you were stubborn, and you refused to take the responsibility for the celestial kingdom we had been building for ages. And you abandoned us." "Yes, yes, I abandoned you, but I had very good reasons to do so." "Reasons?!" Ameris repeats Ardax's words in her mind in a mildly angry voice. It's more a statement than a question and she fidget on her throne. "Talking about the past is pointless. The real question is what we are going to do now." Ardax is thinking for a moment, looking at the crowd waiting for his suggestion.

He frowns a bit and speaks. "I know I let you down when I left. However, it's about time I sat on the throne as there is no other option."

The queen, the king and the whole crowd are shocked. Ardax's words leave them speechless. After a moment, all kings of the heavens move and Ameris says: "It's unbelievable. The situation must be serious when Ardax is accepting the crown of the celestial kingdom after such a long time. And we are glad to accept your coronation offer. I guess you were not ready then but now I can see your determination to take over the responsibility for the celestial kingdom therefore I am announcing that the coronation may take place right away. Please, get everything ready for the ceremony!" says Ameris to all kings and subjects and they get down to work immediately. All faces are astonished and yet elated, like Aras's or Ilemis's who still doesn't understand what she has just witnessed. All that time she had no idea she was talking to the most powerful of the most powerful ones in the celestial kingdom.

 Her fellow female warriors and she are amused.

The shark creatures are celebrating, cheering and these sounds are echoing throughout the oceanic world. Sharks are capable of great joy when they manage to hunt their prey down. They don't like sharing their prey but once their stomachs are full, they respect the hierarchy depending on a social position. Although Ariads have developed to a higher rank, they don't look down on their ancestors therefore the first generation of the sharks, less perfect but very useful and helpful in fights, serves them loyally. You could see that in the duel between Eld and Kalder where the shark played the key role. Ariads are enjoying their prey as usual. They are eating the dead and taking control over those who have survived and are mourning the loss of their king. Neorids don't forget that's why Ariads are now eating also Kalder's family to evoke the fear in other Neorids and prevent them from any rebellion. Neorids will forever be loyal to their king but if they want to stay alive, they will have to serve another king now, the king of Ariads.

Eld Ion makes love with his wife Uri, and they breed another generation of offsprings for the kingdom of Ariads. Uri is pregnant and this worries Lex because his competition in the right for the throne which has been promised to him, is about to be born. Eld Ion is relying on his instinct, and he believes that Lex Ion will be a great king who will be able to rule over the conquered world. However, Lex doesn't want to leave it to chance, he has found his love, and he would like to conceive an offspring and if everything goes well, even more offsprings. Life in this world is very fragile, though, one offspring eats another up and it is the fittest one who will survive. It was like this also when Lex, Eld and other Ariads were born. It is always about the survival of the fittest. This is the reason why Ariads are so strong. And now they are about to meet much stronger enemy if we may call them enemy. The enemy completely different from those Ariads have defeated so far. Eld is looking into the distance and watching another army coming. This giant wave of warriors is led by Uri, his beloved wife and queen of Ariads who oversees militia. They have a new home now, where Neorids used to live before. He has moved his armies because of the strategical position. There is an extremely hard fight ahead of him but if they win, there will be just one predatory enemy left. Alegians.

King Alegon is the dark lord in the depths who has never seen the light, he even hates it. But there is one more enemy in the depths, Feriases, very cruel predators who are protecting Alegians, the realm of darkness in the depths. They have big heads with jaws in shape of four tusks in the mouth. On their heads they have little horns, just like devils. Their figures are robust and muscular, their skin is brown, and they have sharp claws on their hands which can tear any creature into pieces. They have membranes among their fingers and toes, and they are brilliant swimmers. Their weapons are quite simple, mostly they are armed with different harpoons and many cutting weapons of various kinds, and they make them an enemy that no one wishes to fight against. Eld would say that Eliah was the best warrior he has ever met as crossbreeds are able to cause others the greatest troubles whenever they want to. But to have Feriases on your side would be a huge advantage because together with other predators they defeat both crossbreeds and celestial creatures. However, their king Rehat is vague and to say it is possible to negotiate with him would be an exaggeration. Furthermore, to challenge him to a duel is a suicide. All in all, there is just one strategy left, very blurry and unsure. "Hello there. What are you thinking about, father?" asks Lex. He just frowns at him. "I'm glad you've come to me. It was one hell of a fight, what do you say?" "It surely was, but the enemy we are about to meet is definitely the strongest one, stronger than anything else in this world." "Well, yes, they are very strong. How do you think we could win them and make them stand by our side?" Lex dives deep into his thoughts, trying to find a solution there. He can come up with just one answer. "I think we should head on into the darkness, but not with the whole army, just with the tactical one which can do a lot of damage to the place where they live. Once we push them out, they will become vulnerable." Eld smiles at his son and considers his idea. He tells himself that this solution is not that bad. However, he needs to know that even deeper there are darker forces hiding, no weapons are of any use there, there is only untouched world with creatures nobody has ever seen.

The remaining army has reached its destination. Lex immediately rushes to welcome the queen who commands to everyone: "At ease!" They get down from their sharks and the captured ones follow their example, trying to get used to Ariads. "Greetings, mother." Uri raises her head, and she sees her son. She smiles. "My son, I have been so worried about you." "No need, Mum, you know very well we can take care of ourselves." They hug each other unable to let go until Eld himself arrives and interrupts the welcoming. "Enough!" "I've missed you so much," says Uri and she also hugs Eld, wrapping him tightly in her arms and Eld has difficulty breathing. "Oh, Uri, I think we should stop." "But I can't help myself." "Ok, enough, seriously." Using all his inner power he pushes Uri away. She is still unable to get over the long journey and long separation from her loved ones. Ariads are watching the king and queen's warm welcome. Then Eld addresses everyone: "Welcome to this strategical place. Have a rest, my dear warriors, you need to be fresh because this war will be completely different. Only a few of us brave must meet the enemy against whom our strength is not enough, we will need to use our communication skills. So, find your place and relax." The whole expedition heads towards the slightly broken fortress, and those who have been waiting for the whole militia expedition here will warmly welcome their hostile allies. "It's beautiful when our enemies become our friends." "I wouldn't believe it that much, but it's a lovely idea which will work when they meet our real enemy." "Well, as I see it, you have thought it through properly." Uri looks at the thoughtful Eld, but he mentally summons Lex and other senior members of his army. "Everyone, listen to me now. Our next journey is very risky." Everyone looks at him intently. "We will go to Feriases, who will definitely be waiting for us. You will all follow my instructions, and we will survive. You will let me negotiate with them, no one will interfere. Do you understand what I am saying?" The whole group led by Tad, Lex and Et just nods. "Do you really want to go against Feriases with only a small group of warriors?" Uri mutters anxiously. Eld looks at her mysteriously. "Don't worry, Uri, my darling, we will succeed, and we will win the whole war before we rule this paradise world." Uri just looks nervously at her king and doesn't believe his words, but she has to trust him, even though she finds it hard to do, and she hugs him right away. Others are just looking impartially because they understand how risky this expedition is going to be. Eld and Uri kiss each other, then Uri walks over to Lex, who immediately throws himself into a warm embrace with his mother. "Don't worry, mother, we will certainly return." "I trust you all, for my faith has never failed me before." "You see, never lose hope, mother." He kisses her gently on her cheek, then he pulls away and gets on an already restless shark. "Let's go!" Eld orders. He looks Uri in the eye once more, then quickly disappears in the distance, followed by others.

Uri is watching the outgoing expedition sadly and her best friend Tera is comforting her.

The whole celestial world is up and about when the celestial kings have reconnected and met at this significant occasion. The entire celestial world is having a burst of enthusiasm. The celestial beings are having fun, and they are listening to the trumpets of the guards who are announcing the forthcoming ceremony. Ardax is in his room, getting ready for this important moment. His beloved wife is encouraging him with her gentle kisses and hugs. Their small child who will create the future of this kingdom is just smiling. It is a typical childish joy because the child doesn't understand yet the significance of its birth, it doesn't know that it will become a king who will unite the whole celestial kingdom one day. "My king... I can call you my king now." "No, my queen, I will only be your eternal love." "But I like the idea of you becoming my king better." She kisses Ardax on his mouth and feeling encouraged by this kiss, he is overjoyed. Also, the fright from the great ceremony is running out. "Do you know what that means?" "I know, my king, and I will love you forever although I am losing you now. But you have to do this for our own sake.“ Feeling very sad herself, she is persuading her beloved king that he is doing the right thing. “I will love you forever too, but we have to win this war that's why our love won't save us now.“ With deep sadness he is turning to the door and getting ready to stand before the huge crowd. He already knows what he is going to say about his visions. “Go, my king, everybody is waiting for you.“

Encouraged Ardax smiles at his sweetheart once more, looks out of the room where he was preparing, and he can see the huge crowd waiting for him to receive the royal crown of the heavenly world. After a long time, he finally steps out to the space where the kings of the individual celestial kingdoms are already seated on nine thrones. Beneath the thrones a huge crowd of diverse celestial creatures has gathered. They all are roaring and mentally chanting the name of the king who is to take over the kingdom. Queen Ameris stands up, followed by other kings. "Come among us, our future king. Come to us to receive this coronation," queen Ameris invites Ardax, who is approaching the space for the thrones of nine kings with only a very uncertain movement. He walks slowly to the queen, bows to her, and she greets him again, and the other kings join in, bowing respectfully, Talaof as first. Ameris turns to the whole crowd. "Welcome to this beautiful event. Each of you already knows that unfulfilled love will finally be transformed into reality. This love will eventually bring tremendous power to the whole celestial world. Come to us, King Ardax, and receive our crown." Ardax stands before everyone, and Ameris walks up to him to give him a hug. However, Ardax breaks free and only grabs her hand coldly. Ameris just smiles, for her longing desire for Ardax's love has come true. But his love belongs to another woman, who looks at everything with understanding, and is watching with a smile how the desire for a united kingdom is fulfilled. That kingdom which will fill the empty place of domination over this world.

Everyone rejoices and chants the names of the kings who have just risen. Ardax and Ameris are waiting for them, and the other eight kings, who begin the coronation ceremony of the supreme kings, will set up the long-expected order in the whole celestial kingdom. They are both standing in the middle, waiting for Talaof to start it all. He takes a deep breath before his important lecture to all impatient celestial beings. There is still silence for a while, he is enjoying this moment, then begins with the first words: "Dear noble and honorable celestial creatures, as they call us down there in the depths. I welcome you all here, dear ladies and gentlemen. We all have met here because of an especially important moment. This our revered king and this our revered queen will become the long-awaited royal couple of the whole celestial world. The kings of all our kingdoms have come to take an oath and thus to confirm this love between them. This kingdom is based on love and especially on knowledge, but their actions and their decisions will push us forward, and as they direct it, so will we live. They will decide our destiny, but also the destiny of the whole kingdom. That is why I urge the revered king and queen to step out right before me. According to the tradition, one more question remains. Is there anyone who objects to this union and their coronation?" Everyone looks around and just shrugs and shakes their heads. Talaof looks at the whole crowd. "Since no one has any objections to this union and this coronation, the long-awaited destiny of the kingdom can finally be fulfilled." The whole crowd is silently expecting the beginning of the ritual that leads to the coronation and marriage itself. Although they do not know the concept of marriage.

Talaof continues: "Now you will both repeat after me. Understand?" "Yes, we do," they both say unanimously and with a smile. "I, Ardax, king of Assads, receive the crown of the whole celestial kingdom and swear that I will be a good king who honors all living things in this world and will protect it at all costs, even if it costs me my life. I also accept Ameris, who will stand by my side as a queen. We will both rule with love and cherish it. May my life belong to the celestial kingdom. I solemnly swear to everyone." Ardax repeats Talaof's words as an echo. He then turns to queen Ameris, and she repeats the same words of oath. Then Talaof approaches the two crowns beautifully crafted of colored stones. He grabs the first crown of bright red color, shining splendidly in the beams of light. This crown has nine points and is very big. It will decorate Ameris's head. She bows to receive this majestic honor. Then she straightens up and smiles gently at Ardax with great pride. Talaof approaches the second pedestal, raises the second great crown with nine points glowing in light blue angelic color, and places it on King Ardax's head. He bows, takes Ameris by the hand, and their joined hands are raised. "May this kingdom live forever! This kingdom finally has its kings!" King Talaof, one of the chief advisors in the celestial kingdom, exclaims to the whole crowd. The entire kingdom is roaring and enjoying this ceremony. However, Ilemis is already impatient, because she knows that they do not have much time to build up a huge army. She is very worried that Elds will be able to unite the kingdom of predators and immediately set out for the heavens, where at least Eliah's troops will be waiting.

But those may not be able to manage it this time unless they get help of the celestial creatures.

31

The shark creatures are swimming in the darkness, diving into its depths at high speed, led by Eld who is being followed by his son Lex, Et and commander Tad who happens to be also an advisor to the king. The whole group of warriors is rushing into the far-flung corners where the strange creatures of Feriases are already lurking. Feriases are extremely sensitive, and they can smell any creature approaching their territory. Of course, Eld knows that Feriases will be expecting him. The question is whether they won't be killed straight away. But he must try, it is the only way how to get to Alegon, the king of the depths and gain a very strong ally to conquer the celestial world. Suddenly Eld slows down, because he can feel he is getting close to the border, the point of no return. He gestures the others to slow down their sharks and keep diving into the unknown world of the depths very carefully. There is dark everywhere, they can't even see their hands. Suddenly, Eld stops. It is his instinct that tells him to do so. The others stop as well, having no

clue what comes next. The silence gives them the shivers and they are
surrounded by the pitch-black darkness. Eld attempts to use another of
his useful senses, the one he uses so frequently. He knows Feriases
might be anywhere, even behind their backs. He feels they are near; he
grabs is spear and holds his combat position. Others get their weapons
ready too and they follow Eld who is looking intently into the darkness
which is emanating only freezing silence and cold. He knows they are
very close, beyond the border of Feriases' territory and just one step
further and they will be under an attack. He can feel them, but he is
unable to locate them, and others are trying to smell something too.
Then Eld carefully moves forward. At that very moment, a huge army of
disgusting Feriases with the tusks in their mouths emerges out of
nowhere, razor sharp spears aimed directly at them. Eld's army is
surrounded and helpless. Feriases' army is numerous and merciless. Eld
just raises his spear in a vertical position calmly to show that he has not
come to fight, the others obediently follow his example.

One of the most gigantic Feriases suddenly steps forward, armed to the
teeth, and he comes as close to Eld as possible, and Eld feels
uncomfortable. "Why are you here, you filthy jerks?" asks the giant's
voice in Eld's mind. "We have come to ask for king Alegon's blessing,"
Eld says humbly but the giant shows no sympathy. He remains cold and
he is looking Eld into his eyes in this darkness, because the eyesight of
Feriases works a bit differently. They can see in more spectres which
makes them legendary beasts. "What kind of blessing might you get
from the king, you scums?" "We are no scums, your dirty cowardly
bastard!" storms Eld without any fear. His words immediately put all
Feriases into their combat positions but the giant gestures them to stay
calm, hold their positions and do nothing. "I can see how brave you are
but is your son as brave as you?" asks the giant and Eld is furious
because his son means everything to him, and the giant has hit his soft
spot. "My son is the bravest shark creature ever and not even you, dirty
whoreson, can beat him when it comes to bravery!" he shows his teeth
to the giant and they are standing so close to each other that they could
bite off each other's faces out of rage. The giant looks angrily in Eld's
eyes and notices something that worries him greatly. The determination

that lies in Eld's eyes. But he decides that he won't make it easier for Eld — or any Ariads. "All right, you filthy jerk, let's see how brave your son is. He will fight against one of my sons, whom I will choose. And if your son wins, I will let you go and see King Alegon." It is only now that Eld understands that the giant is Rehat, King of Feriases. He hesitates, he has got into a tight spot. He did not see this coming. "Okay, I accept the challenge!" Lex declares fearlessly. "Hush, my son." „Forgive me, father, but it is our only option. There are just few of us here and as I see it, there is nothing else we can do. I accept the challenge." Lex steps forward and he separates both kings, Rehat and his father Eld, from each other. "See, Eld, your son is brave. We'll see if it is enough." "Don't be so sure that you will win." Rehat bursts out laughing, echoed by others. "Please, follow us now or die." It looks like Rehat leaves them no choice. However, Eld knows that his son is rather inexperienced but not hopeless and without any skills. This fight won't be easy because they are going into the dark depths. And there, Feriases are able to kill any creature, stronger or weaker, before it gets the chance to find its feet there. They are plunging deeper and deeper until suddenly it is all right in front of them.

A huge and very dark mountain is emerging. It is inhabited by those darkest creatures whom Eld himself doesn't understand. Everything is pitch-black but their eyes are slowly adapting, and the colorless dark horizon is revealing its incredible beauty. It is hard to believe how much beauty and diversity you can find in the depths of darkness, even without colors. A big group of Feriases is already waiting, leaning against their terrifying spears, but Ariads are shark creatures who don't scare easily. Also, their instinct is of use in the darkness. Feriases are certain that an Ariad can't be a dangerous opponent. However, Rehat doesn't want to leave anything to chance therefore he will choose the strongest opponent to fight against Lex and Eld knows this. They reach the deep and hilly valley where Rehat's sons, Terefat, Petesat, Ceresat and youngest Kyresat are already waiting. They are welcoming their king, and they take a respectful bow. Rehat has always been extremely strict to them, and you can see it from their attitude to the king. Rehat is a tough king, but in these hostile parts of the world it is only the fittest who survive. Therefore, not even the shark creatures are stronger than Feriases here. However, there are even more resistant creatures who rule over Feriases, and they are Alegians.

"Welcome, Father." "Pleasure is all mine, but we have the visitors, and we shall welcome them as is customary with us. One of you will fight to the death with Eld's son. Terefat, you are the eldest, therefore it should be you. You will fight against strong Lex. Get ready, your moment is coming." Terefat looks at everyone in surprise, knowing that the moment of truth is coming, and they will see if he is able to take over the kingdom of Feriases, which king Rehat has held for so long. "Father, I am honored to meet our guest in a battle, and I hope I will not disappoint you." "Well, I hope so too as only the strongest one can rule in this kingdom so it's high time you showed everyone you are worth of the crown." Telefat takes a bow and sets off inside Ferias Mountain to get ready. Rehat turns to the others, raises his both hands above his head and says: "Welcome. You all know that a very honorable guest has paid us a visit. Now we are going to witness an extraordinary event. My son will show us how strong he is and whether he deserves to rule our kingdom. He will fight to death against a noble Ariad warrior, the son of king Eld Ion, Lex Ion himself." He points at Lex who doesn't hesitate a moment and raises his hands above his head... and everyone gives him a bird in their mind. Rehat signs them to follow him to the mountain in the depths, where they are entering through the carved gate. The whole expedition goes through the gate and then it strikes them. A huge crowd of the shadows of the giant beasts are roaring in their minds. The roar of the crowd who believes that their warrior will become the king is almost deafening. Eld and Lex look each other in the eye. Lex grins and then smiles because he knows that only fear will help him defeat the son of such a beast.

Terefat is in the circle, ready for the fight. The whole crowd is standing on their feet in a huge dark arena. Above the arena, there is the audience sitting on the large carved rows running around the whole circle. The rows are on each floor, the floors rise to enormous heights and there are creatures everywhere, encouraging the son of the king of the guardians of the dark depths of Feriases. Terefat is already waiting, standing very calmly in the middle of a circular arena backlit by small fireflies, so that no one is favored in this duel. Ariads are surprised that Feriases are so noble and fair. Nevertheless, the arena is quite dark, but visibility is acceptable to everyone. Terefat is a huge muscular creature holding a spear in one hand in an upright position, as if leaning against the ground, and in the other hand his well-carved serrated sword. His face looks scary with dark yellow pupils in the eyes and dominant tusks in the mouth. And the famous huge head on the top with two arches on the neck and on the sides decorated with layers of wrinkles. He is looking with those wild eyes at his opponent, who is just entering the arena. It is when Eld stops him for a moment, touching his shoulder and looks him in the eyes. "You know what to do. Don't try to kill him straight away. Use his power against him. Don't rush, take it easy, he might be at home here, but it doesn't have to be necessarily an advantage. We have already beaten a lot of our enemies on their own territories, and that is our strength. Patience." Eld's advice encourages Lex, he turns back and enters the arena. "Hm.." Rehat is looking into the ground and shaking his head. „So, the time has come and one of my sons is about to show us how strong he is. He has been through so many trainings and battles. Now he can finally use all his experience and skills in a decisive battle against an enormously powerful opponent Lex Ion. The winner will lead the armies to the war against the celestial creatures who are preventing us from seeing the light belonging only to us. I believe we will finally attack the heavens and conquer them. And we will restore the proper order. May the stronger, better and smarter win," he calls out to the crowd who is cheering and calling Terefat's name.

Terefat raises his hand above his head, the crowd keeps roaring. Lex is standing still and watching Terefat perform. After a while, Eld and Rehat look at each other and nod slightly to start a fight. Rehat calls on both rivals to get ready. They are holding their weapons tightly in their hands and standing in a fighting position against each other. Once more Lex looks into his father's eyes, who telepathically advises him on what to do. After a while, he looks into the eyes of his opponent and squeezes a spear in his right hand and his small sword in his left. Terefat sees his smaller opponent as a scapegoat. It should be easy to defeat him in a duel where no one expects anything other than victory; and that's why Lex has an advantage. Terefat is holding a spear in his hand and briefly checks both of his swords on his back. They are staring at the thoughtful Rehat, who looks at Eld and he just blinks at him to finally start it. Rehat is still looking into the eyes of his son Terefat, a little incredulously, but he is proud of him, because he has heroically set out to fight against one of the strongest warriors, even though Terefat doesn't know it yet. Rehat looks at Eld, smiles, and starts a big fight for everything with a hand gesture.

Terefat and Lex get closer, checking each other a little. Especially Lex, whose eyesight is not so good, but he is used to it, and there are dim lights everywhere, which emit at least a little light in the ominous darkness. Terefat's vision - as with all Feriases - is a little different, evolutionarily adapted to darkness. However, Rehat wanted the fight to be fair, so they are both on the same level. The spectators are chanting, watching the start of the fight with tension. Terefat is the first to try to fight more proactively and tries different combinations of attacks, once with a spear and once with a sword, but Lex reflects it all resiliently and deftly with his weapons, but without a response. He hasn't attacked yet; he is waiting for Terefat's mistakes. Terefat stops for a while and tries to push Lex more to the wall, where he could already be at a great advantage. But Lex is very agile, he avoids each trap. Terefat launches another shower of attacks and gets angry when Lex only repulses them, because he doesn't see any of his attacks and doesn't know how to knock down his defense. "Will you keep defending yourself so cowardly without a fight, or will you finally start fighting like a real warrior?" he asks, angrily attacking Lex also verbally. He looks at his father in a flash, who only reassures him with a smile and signs him to wait. Lex does not react to Terefat's words and maintains a defensive stance, shattering his weapons even more strongly in his hands. Terefat starts bouncing around Lex and continues with another desperate shower of attacks. But Lex has already noticed some of Terefat's soft spots in the attack, and he can see how he could injure Terefat. However, after several attacks, Terefat stops and again tries to push Lex to the wall with his movement, but Lex is still very elegantly resisting Terefat's pressure. He looks into Eld's eyes for a moment and Eld nods slightly. Lex immediately understands. "I don't know how long you want to play like this with me, but I'm very patient and trust me, I will get you sooner or later." Lex smiles inwardly, takes a fighting stance, and looks into Terefat's menacing eyes. He provokes him in his thoughts: "Come on, you ugly monster without a common sense!" Terefat is even more annoyed, he throws a spear at Lex, but he deftly avoids this attack. Terefat draws his second sword and runs to Lex. He starts waving his swords, once his left hand and once his right. Lex again deftly avoids this attack, but suddenly he does something surprising. Instead of stepping back, he presses against Terefat, making an uncomfortable and painful cut on his thigh with his sword, and immediately moves behind his back. With a painful grimace, Terefat turns his face very quickly towards Lex, who is sailing away from him even further. The whole crowd is shocked and stops chanting. Lex stops with only a slight smile on his face and looks into Terefat's eyes, in which he can see a slight despair and helplessness. Terefat's wound on his thigh starts bleeding and it is rising slightly, as if searching for a way out of this circus. And that adds even more to Terefat's helplessness. Rehat is disappointed, too, as if he knew it is awfully bad. He looks at Eld and sees peace and balance in his eyes. He is a strong war personality who can get out of trouble under any conditions. Then Rehat looks at his helpless son, looks him in the eye for a moment, and sends a farewell speech in the thoughts. "The time has come, my son, to prove whether you can save yourself in this lost battle. But don't worry, show your courage and fight for your life. If you survive, you will prove to all of us that your position as a warlord will be deserved. Good luck, my son." After these words, Terefat turns to Lex and looks into his eyes. He sees great peace, balance, and determination in them. "Congratulations, you've done it, but it's not over yet. Show us that you are a king!" He shouts in his thoughts, squeezing his swords tightly in his hands and rising slightly as the water is driving him upwards. Lex also rises higher. Terefat throws both swords at Lex. He managed to avoid them with difficulty — one of the swords scratches his left ear a bit — and responds by throwing a spear at Terefat. He hits him right in the heart. Terefat is sinking slowly and helplessly to the bottom, until his dead body is lying in a slight ball pierced by the spear. Lex doesn't hesitates for a second, he can't break the Ariad tradition. He immediately cuts off Terefat's head. It separates from the neck, slowly searching for a way up, until after a while - just equally slowly with grief – it falls down. The whole crowd, led by king Rehat, is saddened. Lex can't enjoys this victory because he is not on his soil, and Eld himself motions for him to pay homage to Terefat's deceased, floating body. Rehat, though sad, must acknowledge the defeat of his son and fulfil the promise he has made before the fight itself.

He promises to recognize Lex as the leader of an army of predators to fight against the celestial creatures.

32

A great king is looking down from the tallest tower carved out of the mountain which is on the highest place of the oceanic world, right beneath the surface, almost touching the heavens. This tower is called the celestial tower. You can see the whole celestial kingdom from there, this wonderful colorful country living with the entire soul of the celestial creatures. These creatures always admire the beautiful light of the beams of the rising sun. The entire kingdom is on its knees then and absorbs that power of light and the beings take in energy so strong that it enables them to literally move the mountain. They possess enough knowledge to riot against the predators and stop the pillage and foolish killing of living beings just to feed on them and have full stomachs. "Is that right?" Ardax is asking himself and he is receiving the energy of light coming from the rising sun, which is creating various lovely and glittering colors on the horizon. Ameris, standing behind him, is holding his shoulders, and giving him a massage. "I am so happy you've come here, Ardax, my king and my love. I have missed you so much." Ardax is absentmindedly looking through the makeshift carved window from the tower of the celestial mountain. "I am glad you're happy. And I am also glad that you will join me in the fight against the predators." Ameris frowns. "You really want to do that?!" Ardax turns around and looks up at Ameris. "You know very well we have to do it." "Yes, I do. I understand and you know I would happily follow to the ends of earth." "I love that you always keep your promises. I have almost started to believe that the world has become as proud as a peacock." Ameris starts laughing. "There is no need to worry. Our army which has been secretly developing in the other wars, is well trained now." "Is it?" asks surprised Ardax. "What wars are you talking about?" "See, Ardax, my beloved king? You've been hiding in the safe world for so long, but we've been leading wars against the unknown enemy you know nothing about. You will find out very soon and embrace yourself, for this war will be just the beginning of another war for the world dominance." "What beginning? You know something I don't? Tell me!" "Oh, Ardax, you've been gone for so long. And while you were away, a lot of time passed and the king of Ariads was looking for the way how to ambush us. We discovered a place in the heavens. This place will be our shelter if we lose this war. The predators have been trying to get there too, but we've always managed to stop them. It is a marvellous place over the horizon. You'll see, it's a new place even higher above the heavens. We've discovered our abilities to adapt, and they are well developed. We are able to adjust to the new conditions very fast. However, the predators, once they get above the horizon, they die in a moment. But we'd rather not underestimate them. This world is vast, and we can't know whether they haven't settled somewhere else beyond the horizon yet and they may even be preparing an army somewhere in the distant world." Ardax is listening to Ameris's thoughts, and he is astonished. "That's incredible. It means that this world has no borders and if that's true, what's the point in fighting?" Ameris smiles a bit. "There is a point. It's only that our friend Eliah started to be careless, and he knows about our shelter. We've made a deal that if we happen to lose this war, we'll look after his daughter Ilemis.“ Ardax is lost in his thoughts, looking out of the window. What he has just learnt upsets him even more. He lost a lot while he was hiding together with his nation. In fact, this situation plays into Ameris's hands now so that she can wage war with the predators. Suddenly, Ilemis appears in front of the guards and requires talking to the king and queen. "Well, here we go. Ilemis apparently has no idea what surprise her father and we have prepared for her. Let princess Ilemis come in!” exclaims Ameris nonchalantly.

Ilemis entres and comes closer to the king who has just stood up. He turns his face to Ilemis. “My king, forgive me for intervening into your important discussion but you know very well that we are a bit late.“ “Well, isn’t this our impatient Ilemis... Are you so eager to fight?“ laughs Ameris and joins the conversation. The king frowns at her. “Don’t worry, the time has come. My queen and I have just had an important conversation regarding the decisive battle. I will keep my word. Call up the armies of all nine celestial kingdoms!“ orders king Ardax in his mind and the messengers who have been awaiting his commands, leave to announce with their trumpets that the troops should prepare for the battle. Ameris frowns but she doesn’t say anything. She stands up to get ready to lead the army to the war alongside her beloved king whom she grabs and kisses hard on the lips. Ilemis bows her head in embarrassment and looks down. “Go, Ilemis, go and tell everyone to get ready, the time has come.“ Ilemis takes a bow. “Your wish is my command.“ She leaves the king’s room through the carved door and in a floating movement she rushes into her guest room.

"I have a very nice surprise for you," Ameris tells Ardax gently. He is incredibly careful, as if afraid of the surprise. "What surprise?" Ameris just smiles mischievously and with a great squeal she pulls out something that even Ardax himself has no idea what it is. "What is it?" he asks Ameris cautiously. She is keeping her mischievous smile. "Take a good look now," she warns Ardax to prepare him for the surprise. She pulled out a kind of oblong mass resembling some strange algae. It's starting to take shape and miraculously she is suddenly dressed in it. It has turned into beautiful shimmering red armor. Ardax looks at it with his mouth open, he doesn't understand anything. "Oh my god, you did it. You can do the magic tricks." Ameris burst out laughing, the bubbles coming out of her mouth. "No, we have created something that may change into anything. It's captivating and looks alive. It's something we have been created from. However, this appears to be alive, but it isn't." Ardax is confused. "And isn't it dangerous?" "Dear Ardax, my king. Why do you always believe that everything new is suspicious? Take a look and try it on." She takes another similar mass out of the cabinet and hands it to him. Ardax touches it only in disbelief and very cautiously until he finds the courage to catch it. As he is holding it in his hand, it is waving. It is unpleasant and at the same time very scary, when such an inanimate thing is also so alive. "Well, don't worry, stretch it and model it, you'll see how it adapts to your body. We call it living matter, and it's something of us." Ardax then starts playing with it, laughing at how fun it is to play with it. He puts it on himself and begins to control it mentally when it gives in to him and it becomes something incredible. It adapts to his body and stabilizes. The result is amazing. "Perfect," says satisfied Ardax and he nods in agreement. He is dressed in an amazing armor clung to his body as if they were monolithic friends with the matter. Its favorite light blue color shines on it like the sun in the sky. "I'll show you something now, but don't be scared, please," Ameris warns him. She takes out the same, but smaller, rod-shaped mass. It ripples for a while until it becomes a very nicely shaped spear. She throws it at Ardax, but the spear bounces off him. Ardax is frightened, but he is fascinated by all that this kingdom has developed. "This is absolutely amazing. Now I believe we cannot lose this war." "Stop underestimating the predators, they don't lag behind us either, so don't get too excited. It is to some extent our advantage in combat, but they, in turn, have their own destructive weapons, which will be much more dangerous. Remember: When I tell you to do something, you do it. Do you understand me? "Ardax just looks at her. "I know you love me, and you will protect me. But bear in your mind that I will protect you because I swore to it."Ameris just smiles, and small dimples appear on her cheeks and she kisses Ardax on his mouth with a great passion. After a while, they let go and Ameris says: "Now we have a very difficult test ahead of us. Let's get down to it!" Once again, she gently rubs against Ardax and goes outside. Ardax thinks for a moment and then he follows her.

They are swimming out through the narrow corridors. Just one more gate to go through and behind it – in the light that will blind them – there is one huge army of nine kingdoms. Asads are led by Ardax himself and they are dressed in shiny angelic blue armors. When Ardax joins them, his beloved Xetis is already waiting. "My heart hurts when I see you leave into such a dangerous battle." "Don't worry, my dear, we are ready to defeat them." He looks at Ameris. "But in case I arrive you have to listen to me and follow me straight away. Do you understand?" Xetis is looking at Ameris, but Ameris just grins and looks into her eyes angrily. Then Xetis again turns to Ardax who is getting on his dolphin and hands him the child. Ardax kisses his son on his cheek and then he kisses Xetis passionately. "Fear not, everything will be all right." Ardax looks at all the armies and he checks *Barelians* first. It is a very lazy army, but they can be useful because they are able to come up with excellent strategies. Their silver armours blind him for a moment but then his eyes get used to it. Barelians are a bit shorter with an oval figure and their gills are on their mouths. They are not those most beautiful beings. Just like each celestial creature, they also have well developed membranes among their fingers and toes. They are ruled by Kretion who happens to be the most robust and scariest one of them. *Cesnians* – Ameris grins at Ardax and nods slightly. Their armors are bright red and as an army they are very pushy, and they are not afraid of any danger. Their task has always been to protect the heavens. They are taller and slimmer. Majority of them are women but men are excellent protectors of this kingdom, they are agile and fast warriors. They use javelins as their weapons. Their faces are beautifully developed, and they care about their appearance. The braids on their heads only adorn them like makeshift hair. *Detasions* also have genuinely nice and athletic figures. They are bright green color. They were the ones who opposed this war the most. They are brilliant healers of the injured and wounded but they can also fight when necessary. Their king Oberon is handsome and smart, with nice facial features and slim and flexible figure but just like all the other Detasions, he is very short. The others look similar and there are aso a lot of pretty women among them, very gentle and smiley. Then there are *Glasions* – their king Vahad is a strong man, famous for his light white color. He is well-built and he evokes everyone's respect. The army is very shiny, and they are very exceptional. They are strong but they are especially perfect at entertaining others and making up different technical elements such as weapons and constructions also in less favorable conditions. This might be quite useful in this battle. Queen of *Fenisiats*, Meliterian, is a very fiery lady, pretty and well-built and she can use her female side to her advantage. The women are taller, but slim and agile. It is mainly a female kingdom full of gorgeous women who are irresistible. But this image is deceiving. They can be dangerous in fight and very insidious. They wear pink armor, and they are ready to fight anytime and anywhere. They use mostly swords and axes. The King of *Gavelians*, Talaof, is more of a spiritual mind, and the whole kingdom is more spiritual, focusing on faith and morals. Their brown color makes them one of the dullest of all the celestial armies. Everyone sees this army as useless, because their short statures are not strong, but their thinking and ability to invent any technical thing will be particularly useful. But - and this is especially important - they are very capable in boosting morale. Then there are *Harasets*. Their queen Retiana is very mysterious, only a little is known of her. They are something like special troops of the celestial kingdom. They are brilliant spies, and they excel at assessing individual strategies of fight and terrain where the fight takes place. This queen is noticeably quiet, but she looks fabulous. Her black armor makes her even more beautiful, she has lovely hips and muscular figure, although she is not very tall. Their domain is a perfect adaptability to the changes in strategies of the fight, they can use any weapon and make also a makeshift one if needed. When it comes to the fight, they know no boundaries and they despise the rules which they can change any time, but they are very loyal to the celestial world. They have contributed to the construction of the world the most. Retiana is a close friend of Ameris, she is her eyes and ears together with her mostly female army. And finally, there are *Karions*. It is a golden army. Their king Achas oversees the guards and militia. They are particularly good at defense, especially at exit strategies if something unexpected happens. It is a backup army. They are the strongest and most agile warriors in the whole celestial kingdom, well-built, muscular, and tall. They are great fighters from up close and at a distance too. In this battle, they will be used mainly to destroy the enemy from a distance, because they are also fully accurate and can effectively hit distant targets. They use adapted firearms for this, which are dangerous and can destroy walls, using huge boulders.

Ameris approaches thoughtful Ardax. Xetis walks away, they both look at each other again, but this time Ameris is nice to her and greets her. She then turns to Ardax, who is about to address the army. "Are we all ready to fight for our world and for our freedom?" He asks everyone to prepare them for a difficult journey into the unknown. Everyone exclaims with a determined voice, as if in one voice: "Yes!" Ardax, the king of the whole kingdom of heavens, smirks and says: "May fate be in our favor! Let's fight!"

And they all, like a single cell, are walking into the unknown world of the dark depths.

33

Rehat, King of Feriases, is grief-stricken but he must accept the defeat of his son. The entire kingdom must do so, although unwillingly, because the rules have been agreed and they must be honored by all predators. Eld and other warriors from the kingdom of Ariads are immensely proud of Lex but this journey isn't over and Eld knows it very well. Rehat approaches the group of Ariads with an upset and angry expression in his face. "It's hard for me to accept this defeat but we have a deal, and I will honor it. Your journey continues further, I will personally take you to Alegon, the king of Alegians. But don't get your hopes up because Alegon himself has predicted that my son will be defeated and killed in the fight against your son, I just found it impossible to believe. Alegon is expecting you and he'll surely be glad if Lex himself together with you, Ardax, will lead the army against the celestial creatures up to the heavens. We are ready but we need Alegon's blessing. Come with me. There is the most horrifying adventure lying ahead of you, the one you've never experienced before. These depths are truly terrifying, full of those weirdest creatures you've never had a chance to see elsewhere. This way." Rehat tells Eld who is accompanied by his most loyal guards. "Lead us, Rehat, king of Feriases and we will follow you," shouts Lex. It seems that his self-confidence has boosted up to the heavens he wishes to conquer so much. Rehat grins at everyone and starts swimming. Others are right behind him.

They are swimming for a moment in the darkness along a deep mountain area on the plain, and then they find an abyss and when they look into it, they shiver with fear. They stop on the edge for a while. Everyone is almost hypnotizing the darkness from the depths before they decide to go into that terrifying world. Even the cruel and fearless predators themselves are scared to death, because these depths are infamous for various myths and legends that do not lag behind reality. "Let's go, that is if you haven't had a change of heart because once you descend into those depths, there will be no way back." Rehat hesitates a moment and then he sets off to those pitch-black depths, followed by frightened warriors. Ariads can't see anything but Feriases' eyes are adapting to the darkness. Their vision might be a bit blurry, but they are alert because they could be attacked by any vermin who have no mercy on others. These vermins are ruled by Alegon himself, they supply him with food constantly but now Alegon might need their services so the situation is playing into their hands and the danger shall be eliminated. However, this doesn't need to apply to everyone. They are getting deeper and deeper into the darkness. They feel even bigger pressure and the deeper they get the more intense it gets. Although these creatures are adapted to this like almost every predator, but the bodies are not yet adapted to heavenly life. Especially King Alegon is cursed because he can't leave the depths. He is fed by darkness and pressure; he would die instantly if he emerged. The darkness is getting darker and darker as they sink, they can't see their hands, but they already feel as if something is watching them and moving around them. Eld and the others already intuitively feel their surroundings, they feel that they are approaching the kingdom of Alegians.

They keep swimming when suddenly they can hear some hissing and feel a wave which gently touches their bodies. The hissing gets stronger and out of the blue a huge mouth of a dark boa appears right in front of Rehat and everyone is frozen stiff with fear. They are surrounded by plenty of boas. The one standing in front of Rehat and hissing seems to be smiling and then he talks to them in their minds: "Well, well, our king is already expecting you. Don't get us wrong, we would eat you up, but we can't, you are way too important for us. Be silent, speak only when you are asked something. Now, follow us." The boa teaches them good manners customary in king Alegon's kingdom. Then he turns around and leads them a bit further into the depths of Alegians' realm where a great surprise is waiting for them: The kingdom is built from a huge mountain of stones. This mountain is carved into the beautiful fortress. It is a kind of poorly built palace, but it is lovely and dark.

They step inside through a cold gate, and they meet crowds of various kinds they have never seen or heard of before. They are dark creatures living in the depths, some of them have both hands and fins and they are female and male. Some of them have hands and legs and on the big heads the sprouts looking like tentacles of an octopus. This world is surprisingly varied provided they live in such hostile environment. They are diving deeper and deeper into the fortress, but their eyes have already got used to the darkness. They can see a lot of chambers and wide alleys among them, and they get to the vast elliptical room which has an equally vast terrace. And on it they glance Alegon, standing on a sort of platform. He has a very robust, oval and muscular figure and he is surrounded by different pretty women, his concubines, who have the small lumps instead of hair on their heads, reminding of braided hair. Their faces are beautiful and symmetrical, but their snake tongues are a bit repulsive. They have nice straight teeth. They are just having a delicious lunch. Their servants are bringing food which they have managed to catch. In addition to being very robust and muscular, Alegon's head is proportioned to the body, and it is sinewy, very symmetric and veined. It's a sort of ugly beauty with the sprouts on the head, also looking like braids. His fiery red eyes are literally lighting up the surroundings and they've earned a big respect. Everyone is afraid of him because he is immortal, and nobody knows how he managed to achieve that.

Alegon is staring at the guests for a while and then he bursts out laughing: "I had no idea that even fearless Ariads can get so scared. How do you want to win this war when you are so afraid? Come and join us, you are our guests after all, aren't you?" Everyone feels relieved when Alegon himself asks them to join him. The boa just nods his head and encourages them to follow the king, then he turns around and goes outside to keep on guarding the vast kingdom of depths. They all enter the royal room of Alegon, who is surrounded by pretty concubines, and they are about to have a word. They feel honored because even Rehat himself rarely visits this place and he can't find it on his own without being accompanied by boas. However, although he belongs to the first line of the guards of the depths, each time he comes here, he feels very frightened and full of respect. Someone simply must be at the edge of the darkness. They enter the room through the small gate, and they have to go along the corridor which winds up. They are welcomed by a lot of wonderful dark women with braids in their heads living in a harem. They have tiny membranes among the fingers. "It's interesting that even in the world like this you may encounter such stunning ladies," says Eld whose fear might have gone, but he still feels a great respect. He approaches Alegon who is almost three heads taller let alone being thrice as wide and strong. Alegon starts laughing again and then he welcomes his guests. "Well, the rumor has it the dark world is a terrible place but it's not that bad in the end. However, what I desire is to see the celestial world. I've heard so many lovely legends and myths about it that my desire has become my ultimate target." Alegon and he shake hands and then he greets Rehat. "Well, Rehat, my friend, you've completed your task but now you have to excuse us. Please, leave us alone." Rehat looks at Eld and Alegon enviously, but he has to accept this and he leaves. Obviously, what they are going to talk about is very confidential and only those who will lead the allied army into the great battle for the world dominance have the right to know the secret. Lex passes by, being watched by Alegon who is smiling proudly.

Alegon opens his arms and expects to hug Lex Ion, the son of king of Ariads. "Well, here comes our future and salvation who will lead this big war." Lex lets Alegon hug him and surprised Eld just nods and signs him not to worry and do what the king of the darkness wants him to do. They hug tightly and then Alegon checks him out with his hands on Lex's shoulders and hugs him again as if he was his own son. He lets go of him after a while and he asks them both to take a seat on a rocky bench where they are immediately surrounded by the beautiful concubines, and they start flirting with them. Alegon turns his throne inwards, and he also sits down on it. Most of the time his throne is turned outwards to the terrace, where you can see the whole swarming dark kingdom inside a huge rocky fortress. In front of the room there is large space where all dark creatures usually gather to listen to Alegon's lectures, which bring them a lot of fun. He sits down on the throne and his beautiful concubines sit on his knees. Then come the servants with lots of quality goodies for the guests. "I'm very happy to finally have a peaceful meal, my friends. Take this treat as a gesture of my respect for you. You are precious to me. Let's forget about a very instructive battle we lost. We were not prepared for our very advanced enemy. I've learned my lesson from this defeat, and as I see it, so have you." Eld looks into Alegon's eyes, which directly hypnotize him. He tries to read his mind, but he doesn't succeed, Alegon is too mature for that. He gives up, smiles, and looks at excited Lex. But he himself is incredibly careful. Alegon also looks Elder in the eye with a slightly forced smile. "My son and I are excited about your hospitality, and it is very nice that you have also given us a little pleasure, but I think we should move on to more serious topics that are important for our progress. Your blessing and support for this war are essential, and I think that with this little treat, we are just wasting time that we could use more effectively. With all due respect to you," Eld finishes with a serious face. Alegon is just amused. He grins and shows his pretended smile again. "Hm, I appreciate your sincerity, Eld. You are the one who has suffered the most of us all. You fought against Eliah in a direct combat, which certainly provided you with a lot of experience. But don't worry, I won't leave you alone, not one of you. After all, we're not just allies, we're friends." Eld laughs. Lex frowns at his father, because he doesn't understand exactly what he's talking about when he treats Alegon like this without respect. But he trusts his father and his instincts. When Eld stops laughing, he puts on his serious face again and now stares even harder into Alegon's eyes. "I passionately believe that this will not be the same as the last time when your army withdrew and fled like the greatest cowards in the world. Even those little peaceful cowards, whom I love to enjoy as dinner, are braver than your cowardly useless warriors. If such a situation occurs again, I will kill anyone who retreats. Do you understand, Alegon, my king?"

Alegon frowns a bit more, he leans against the throne and canoodles with his concubines a little. "Now you got me. You know very well, Eld, that you are the one I appreciate the most and I understand your anger but then we weren't strong enough to defeat such a powerful army. Now the situation will be different, and I believe we will beat them. Listen to me carefully. You don't understand things like tactics and thinking. It won't be just a classic battle. This battle will be only the beginning." Eld raises his eyebrows, having no idea what Alegon has just said. Lex also stops canoodling with the concubines when he hears Alegon's words that have upset Eld even more. "Ok, is there something I don't know about? Stop beating around the bush and just say it. There are too many things you've been hiding from me, I feel. And that's not nice." Alegon remains calm, and he starts laughing a little to show he has the upper hand when it comes to the information. "Well, Eld, there is nothing to worry about, this battle will help you understand. All I can tell you is that it didn't end with that famous war which is now the thing of the past. Another one started, the war for the celestial world. I know we wouldn't survive a second there, but we've found out that the celestial creatures are very adaptable, and we'd never win this battle for the heavens. However, after a long time of adaptation we'd be able to tackle these adverse conditions. That's why I want to wait until the celestial beings come in time to fight against us. So, our tactics, or my tactics if you wish, is to draw the celestial beings into the war because they have something what we need to get. It could help us solve our problem with the hostile celestial conditions."

Eld is taken aback and even more puzzled than before. "Brilliant. I don't understand anything, and I don't know why I've been leading this war when we are going to lose it again and a lot of our warriors are going to die. What on earth might the celestial beings have that you wish you had it too?" Alegon bursts out laughing haughtily. "What I want is what they are wearing. Come, follow me, I'll show you a weapon that will work against their armors." Alegon stands up and swims out of the room. Eld and the others swim after him with great interest. They are swimming towards another chamber where Alegon is hiding precious jewels. Feeling very curious, Rehat asks: "What's going on?" His question remains unanswered, everyone is heading noisily to the chamber across the whole square. The chamber is large and beautifully decorated with different carved spurs and statues of various unknown personalities that no one has seen ever before. They are a bit damaged, as if cut with different cutting objects. Elated Alegon stops at one of the small chests and takes a strange object out of it. Then he approaches one untraditional spear ended with unusual and dreadfully looking serrated blade. Alegon is looking at Rehat, but he says nothing, because this war will concern him as well. Then he looks Eld in the eyes and his gaze meets his son's too. "Hm, I can see the questions in your eyes and how eager you are to find out what it is I wanna show you. We've been at war with the celestial beings for ages and we've learnt something. We've discovered their very unusual armor we were unable to destroy, and they kept beating us again and again. Now we know how to deal with it.“ He stretched the small object as wide as possible and put it on one of the statues. “Eld or Lex, please be so kind and grab a spear and throw it at this statue, especially at the cloth I’ve just stretched over it.“ He pointed at the stand with the spears and Lex takes his chance immediately, impatient to know what this is all about.

He pulls out one of the spears and weighs it in his hand for a while. Alegon is watching him with a smile. “Come on, throw it at that statue,“ he encourages him again. Lex just grins, shrugs his shoulders, and throws the spear at the statue. The spear is flying through the water, hits the statue and breaks. Everyone is astonished, and Eld can’t believe his eyes. “What is this? Is this their armor? And we are supposed to fight against them?“ Alegon only smiles a little and he tries to calm them down. “Fear not. It may seem hopeless now. I won’t waste any more time explaining. Each battle that we lost taught us something and made us stronger. They have no idea that with each battle we become more mature and powerful. After a lot of struggles and a great coincidence we managed to get a piece of their armor. What is more, we managed to create an anti-weapon. It is effective, but we must be perfectly accurate because for some reason it doesn’t work every time. It might be because they are improving their armors as well. You need to be standing really close if you want it to work. Eld, be so nice and throw this spear I am handing you at that statue.“ Alegon approaches Eld and hands him the spear. Eld checks it, weighs it with curiosity and suddenly throws it at the statue. The spear is making its way through the thick waters, it sinks into the statue and half of it comes off. The crowds cheer. Eld is looking at Alegon with a smile and Alegon smiles back. “So, you believe me now, Eld, king of Ariads?“ Eld isn’t able to hide his excitement and he comes closer to Alegon. “My king, have you got many such weapons ready for the decisive battle? This is my question for you.“ Alegon smiles, looks at all those creatures who believe in victory over the celestial creatures and shakes Eld’s hand.   “Of course, we do. But there is one thing you always need to keep in your mind: These weapons are effective only in a close combat." Eld smiles darkly. "I do get it. And that's more than enough." "Well then, shall we begin the war?" "We shall."

They shake their hands firmly, full of hope for success.

Eld is sitting on his shark who is fidgeting impatiently and floating in front of a huge army waiting for his speech that shall motivate them to fight this crucial battle against the celestial creatures. Eld is thinking about Alegon's words all the time. This battle won't be only about the victory of the predators over the celestial creatures but also about gaining a very precious loot. Eld is considering everything, and he decides to keep this card up his sleeve as a kind of triumph that he is expected to bring Alegon himself. Alegon obviously cares more about the precious loot than the victory which Eld finds rather worrying but there's nothing he can do about it now. He takes his time, then he looks at his army that is to be led by his son Lex. Lex is hugging and kissing Era and they are whispering farewell words to each other. His friend Et is standing behind him and Tad is patting his shoulder. It's a great honor for Lex to be standing in front of the army and he is waiting for his father to begin. He wishes to reach a great success so that his father could be proud of him. Just Uri is watching her loved ones with big worries. She's afraid she is going to lose one of them. Her militia is a bit jealous. They can't take part in the battle despite being very well-trained. After what seems to be ages, Eld delivers his speech. "Welcome, the army of brave allies. Your time has come, and you can prove you deserve your freedom. The freedom that you will get only when you prove your loyalty to me. It's your loyalty that will help us win this war against the celestial creatures. I know some of you hate me, but this hatred is pointless now, since our enemy is up there, and he is our greatest threat that may terminate our existence. You must understand this. Your cowardly kings who have deserted the fight and brought you your defeat are not here anymore. You are fighting for us now. And if I say you will fight, you will do your best even if it costs you your life. If you fight as I expect you to, you will be rewarded. I promise. However, if you act cowardly, you will be executed, and we'll eat you as a dessert. Do you understand?" The whole army shouts like one: "We do!" Eld grins and enjoys this miraculous moment. It feels amazing to have an army ready to die in this fight. "Well then, let's hesitate no more. Let's fight!" The words are echoing in the warriors' minds. Eld turns around and heads forward on his shark. He is being followed by his army at the sound of noise and whirl of dust as if it was a huge dragon.

Eliah and the small group are waiting on a gigantic artificially made cobweb on the place where one fight already took place. They are recalling those moments in their minds. Eliah keeps staring up and he is impatiently waiting for so much needed reinforcements. "Where are our celestial friends?" the commander of his troop, Derieh, keeps asking him. Eliah gets angry. "Why do you keep asking me the same thing over and over again?! Don't you trust my daughter? Don't you trust the heavens and my brother whom we honor so much? They will be here in time." He spurns his friend disdainfully. Then he focuses on the depths, trying to see whether something is coming out of there. After a moment he can feel a shiver, a kind of anxiety of his dolphin that accompanies him in each of his battles. The shiver is getting more and more intense and other Eliah's warriors are feeling it now too. Derieh attempts to approach him again, but this time Eliah gestures him to be quiet and hold on. At the same time, he waves his hand and signals his army to scatter around and get the firing arms famous for their destructive power ready. In the meantime, he keeps on focusing, as if he was hypnotizing the depths, trying to persuade the army of the predators to stay where it is a while longer. However, the noise and rumble are getting stronger, they can hear the war drums and trumpets telling them "We, the dark creatures from the depths, are coming!" Eliah looks up at the heavens but no sign of any movement there. Then he is gazing into the depths again and he can feel the fear overcoming him. Suddenly small trolls appear. They are wandering around, observing the entire mountain reaching up into the heights connected to the celestial world. Eliah orders everyone to do nothing. He knows these trolls are the scouts from the depths. The rumble is even more intense now, it is turning into thunder of the drums and sirens and pretty soon, the wave hitting everything and signaling the arrival of the army of the dark creatures is not only heard but also seen. Suddenly it appears on the horizon and Eliah already knows that if reinforcements do not come, they have truly little chance against such a monstrous and huge army.

Suddenly, near a spider's web, Eld gestures for his army to stop. As usual, he looks into the distance and hypnotizes the terrain ahead. The whole army is silent in surprise. "There's no one here?!" Everyone wonders as they look up at the sky, into the void that seems to be smiling at them. The little light behind the cobweb is still there. "Nothing has changed here," Eld says to himself, and his impatient white shark moves nervously under him. Eliah and the others are just looking around helpless, hidden, and scattered all over the web. "Where are our allies? Have they just cowardly left us at the mercy of these ferocious predators?" Everyone is asking. Eld continues staring into the distance as his son and commander approach him. "What's going on here? Is it supposed to be a joke, or is it a trap?" Eld signs him to keep quiet and using his very secretive mind voice he tells him to keep a close eye on the distance at the height where the little light is visible. Suddenly a small bubble appears, descending directly to Eld and his son, and it strokes his face. Eld can feel the little ripple, the faint tremor that intensifies more and more. Eliah and his entire small army feel this too, and they tell each other: "There is nothing to worry about. The reinforcement is coming." They are relieved. It is approaching, that cell of celestial creatures who have come to fight for their honor and protect life more valuable than anything else. That wave is followed by another and another, the waves are intensifying and signaling that the celestial creatures are on their way. You can already hear the battle trumpets, spreading the sound through the whole heavens, as an echo saying: Creatures of darkness, we are coming, just wait for us. It will be a huge army, everyone thinks. The smallest, tiny scouts appear, noting with their little snouts that reinforcements are already here. The rumble of the celestial creatures makes it clear that there is no going back, the dark creatures say in their minds, and they are waiting for Eld's instruction to Lex, the commander of the armies of the dark creatures from the depths. At that moment, a huge army of nine heavenly kingdoms, led by Ameris and King Ardax, emerges from behind the little light. Ardax waves his hand and halts his army near the border between the depths of darkness and the world of heavens.

And the army that has just emerged from under that little celestial light stops.

Two armies are standing on the border which separates the world of depths and the world of heavens. They are observing each other and waiting for a battle that will determine the fate of the world and the direction it will take. Will it be the world of constant survival of the fittest and eating up the others or the world of peace and eternal welfare, acquiring the knowledge about itself? Ameris is looking into the distance and watching her enemy Eld Ion from behind the mask. She's been dreaming about killing him for so long. Her animosity and desire for revenge are still present and it doesn't make her one of the most peaceful creatures ever. Eld is calmly checking out everyone when he notices Ameris looking at him. Eliah appears on the border. The eyes of two unforgettable rivals who haven't finished their duel for life and death meet. Eld strokes his wound which is a reminder of that duel. The duel which has taught him so much and reminds him of the fact that with every single victory there is still so much to work on. Eliah runs along the border very swiftly and bounces off up to the celestial army to welcome them. Ardax calms down his own army and tells them to hold their positions. Only Ilemis and her female guardians step out of the row to welcome their king. Ameris picks up her mask to reveal her face and greet Eliah, who has swum up to them. They all are indignantly watching Eliah approach the army of the warriors of nine celestial kingdoms. "It's a great honor to see you here. You've kept your word, and I am going to keep mine. We are right where we left off but now, we will start the war that will decide the fate of us all." Ardax grins and looks into his brother's eyes. He gets down of his dolphin and hugs Eliah. "The pleasure is all mine. I am honored to be able to fight by your side, brother. I like you very much and it's great to see you after such a long time." Finally they let go of each other. Meanwhile they are approached by Ilemis who jumps into her father's arms. "You've accomplished your mission, and I am very proud of you, my girl. Now step back." Ilemis pulls away reluctantly from her father and frowns. "Not a chance. I'll fight alongside all of you." "Out of the question." "Give her a break, Eliah, we could use any help we may get because this is the fight of all of us. If we lose now, we'll lose everything," intervenes Ameris and Eliah frowns at her. "You know what we've agreed on and I expect you to honour our deal." Ameris grins and smiles a bit. "I will keep my word, but I won't stand up against the will to fight for all of us. I'll protect your daughter, but I won't keep her from fighting. She'll be our backup together with Aras and I believe this is a nice compromise."

Eliah doesn't like it at all. He turns to the depths as if searching for his enemy Eld, who has been watching the celestial army from his depths all the time. He is staring into the depths until he catches Eld's gaze who is just sending the mind message to the celestial creatures. "I can see you all, celestial creatures. I won't negotiate with you. We are here to slaughter you all. And I am especially looking forward to killing you, Eliah, when we meet in a direct fight. You've taught me a lot and I learnt my lesson after our last duel ages ago. And now, in this battle, you'll die by my hand." Eliah bursts out laughing, his laughter is echoing among all the warriors on this soil. "I like your optimism resulting from the last battle, I really do. However, I've been training hard too, and I truly believe you won't run away from this fight like the greatest coward. I am more than ready to cut your head off. I may have been a little inexperienced then, but you won't survive this battle." Having heard Eliah's words, Eld laughs loudly and after a while he orders: "Lapads, shoot!!!!!" Out of the blue, something is rolling loudly from the depths. They are huge boulders flying towards the firm cobweb which has been protecting the celestial world all the time. Eliah manages to scream out: "Fire, brothers, fire!!!" and the defense on the cobweb launches the covering shots.

The huge boulders are rolling but most of them fall apart under the fire of big oblong stone arrows. Just a few of them find their way into the stone net that shakes after having been hit strongly. Ameris immediately issues a new order: "Support the cover fire, Karions!" When everything storms, king of Karions, Achas says: "Shoot, my brothers!" The big army joins them at once with their firearms which are turning from the small pieces of unusual matter into gigantic monsters. Eliah is speechless. Ilemis joins him out of the blue and they start shooting their arrows to eliminate the fire of boulders launched by Lapads. Eliah is proudly looking at his daughter who shouts in her mind: "Keep shooting! Don't stop!" Everyone is shooting at will but there are more and more boulders rolling, hitting the wall which won't resist much longer. Observing the surroundings, Ardax can see that the net will go loose soon, and the enemy will then focus on its soft spot. Eld is watching this performance with a calm expression on his face. Lex, who is standing next to him, looks anxious but Eld encourages him to maintain his balance and do nothing. It's obvious that nobody wants only to watch the shooting but there is not much they can do unless the defense isn't weakened a little and they can start fighting man to man. And this is one of the predators' strengths.

The celestial creatures have no idea what threat they are about to face.
The entire army scattered in the net is shooting into the depths where
the predators ready to fight are hiding. Eld is still holding them back but
some of them are way too impatient and they are immediately punished
for this when they are torn into pieces. The pieces of their bodies are
found all around and Lex and Et look at Ed. He tells them: "See? Do you
understand now why it is important to wait?" Needless to say, when the
others see the pieces of the bodies sinking into the depths, they are
scared enough, and they are waiting. They have a huge firing force
because they've come up with an invention which is continuously
drilling the boulders out of the depths where there are enough stones.
The sharp boulders are mined and ready to be fired. However, the
celestial creatures are not having a rest either, the sources of their stone
matter are unlimited. When they meet their target, they crush it
immediately.

Eld is watching the net, and he notices a small crack which gives him
hope in this hard duel of shootings. His mind issues a new order to aim
the shooting at that place. The signal slowly gets to Lapads and their
guides who begin to aim them in the desired direction. Most of the
shooting is aimed at the crack. Ardax gazes into the space where
everyone is focused on the cover shooting and catches the sight of that
not very small crack. He shouts in his mind and alerts everyone to this
danger. The cover shooting starts to focus on the protection of that
crack, but Aras tells him it's pointless because cracks are now emerging
also elsewhere. Ardax summons the kings of the celestial armies.
Everyone is in the back and safe, Ameris, Ardax, Eliah, Aras and other
kings. Ilemis notices this but she leaves them alone as she knows it is
important to morally support the fire of continuously rolling boulders
now, destroying the barrier between the dark and celestial world.
Gavelians, led by Talaof, offer their moral support to the troops and
Talaof begins to blow the trumpet even harder. Oliaf also approaches
her and helps her with shooting. Ilemis smiles kindly at Oliaf and
continues to shoot, supported by the energy of Oliaf's love. "What do

you think of what's going on in the background where the kings are?" Ilemis keeps on shooting, and she catches Oliaf's thought, then turns to him. "Don't expect anything good. Prepare for the worst, because when our kings meet in the background, it is never a good sign." Oliaf looks at the meeting of the kings again and looks into Aras's worried eyes. "I think it's time to prepare for a direct combat, because this depth fire is very effective and continuous." "Well, did you really think you wouldn't encounter the predators in a duel? You probably haven't learnt from the past, and that's a mistake, because the predators have prepared very well and learnt from their mistakes. Eld took revenge on all the traitors and reunited the predators, who, even with great reluctance and pressure, are fighting by his side. If they do not obey him, they will die, but if they win, they will be rewarded with so-called freedom. So, don't expect any retreat from the predators now. We all have to fight, but we have one advantage, an escape to the safety of the celestial world where the predators can't follow us." Ardax looks thoughtfully at Ameris, Eliah, and the others. "I can see an agreement here that I didn't know about. And not many beings knew about it, so explain to me now what's going on here." All kings and others look at each other and then they look at Ameris. She doesn't feel very comfortable and finally she says: "I am very sorry to tell you that when the predators manage to get through our net, we'll be very vulnerable. Therefore, I highly recommend we all should set out to our new world. There we'll have enough time to get ready for another war against the predators." She is looking at Ardax but he has no idea what Ameris is talking about. "I know that you don't understand anything, my dear Ardax, but when I tell you to, you will set out. You will set out immediately, no questions asked. Achas will protect you and so will the backup troops. The predators might win this battle, but not the war." "I don't understand a thing, but I can see you haven't come here to win. I don't intend to give up this fight, so heads up and let's fight to defend our net." Everyone grins but they listen to Ardax and they follow him to help defend that fragile stone net.

Ilemis and Oliaf are sturdily shooting at the flying boulders, but the rocks always find their way. Everyone aims at the soft spots in the net, and it is only the matter of time when the net tears apart. Eld is waiting patiently, the boulders keep rolling. The net is about to get loose. Suddenly he can see one crack getting bigger and bigger. One huge boulder has found the way towards it and crashed into it. And then it happens. The net rips and collapses like a house of cards. There is a large hole now which is opening the door for the predators to enter the celestial world. Ardax looks Ilemis into her eyes and then he finds Ameris's look. Then he signals with an eloquent gesture that a large part of the army shall move and defend the route that has been created for the predators. Eld shouts in his mind: "Start fighting, everyone!"

And the trumpets sound to the depths of darkness.

The huge boulders are flying out of the depths towards the crack that is opening the predators the way into the celestial world. They are rolling at the calm pace, finding their way into the hole. The boulders are not only going to destroy, but they are also bringing the unwanted passengers. Bombarding them seems to be pointless, those huge boulders have found their way and caused a massive destruction inside the cobweb where the defense is desperately shooting back. As soon as they have crashed, the malicious monsters of a snake origin fly out of them and attack immediately. They are hissing terribly and shouting, holding the special spears in their hands. And as if this is not enough, Eliah's army is dying in these fierce attacks. But the bravery of this army is obvious, and they won't give up so easily. A lot of blood will flow all around in this chaotic struggle for positions. More boulders find their way in, and more monsters emerge. The brave fighters are defending themselves, shooting and fencing face to face with monsters, but it's in vain. These attacks are causing more and more damage. If help does not come, the monsters will spread very quickly into a cobweb, which forms a protective barrier against the predators. Fencing and fighting for their lives, they are surprised that the weapons of those monsters are so effective. Suddenly, however, a huge reinforcement arrives, Aras, Eliah, Ilemis and Oliaf at the head of a large army begin to fight and defend the huge breakthrough that has created a path of hope for the predators into the celestial world. More boulders and more monsters arrive, with Eliah cutting one monster after another into pieces with his sword. Limbs are flying all around and the bloody environment obscures the view from the warriors, but the monsters are just constantly emerging from this bloody thicket. Ilemis and Oliaf and Arasus kill them one after another with the help of a large army willing to die for their celestial kings. Eld calls again to his other allies to get ready. He knows exactly what the bloodthirsty monsters want. They are hungry for prey, then even the fear will pass. More boulders are rolling, and the defenders are shooting at them in vain, because always a few of them get into a breakthrough and something peels off the cobweb again.

The boulders are crashing and whirling the dust all around. Aras looks at Eliah who is helplessly staring at his daughter Ilemis who is looking lovingly into Oliaf's eyes. Then he looks at Aras. "Am I missing something?" Aras shakes his head as if he was giving up. "Don't ask me, I know nothing." Oliaf is trying to get out of it. At that very moment the giant crocodiles appear, and they are attacking them together with their warriors. Oliaf is disgusted. "I can stand anything except for these annoying crocodiles. I hate them." Ilemis and the others are killing one monster after another, but they know one thing: They need to abandon their position because these monsters will outnumber them very soon. They are reversing and Eliah screams out: "Retreat!" And everyone backs off into the space from where there is one tunnel after another until they get to the celestial world. Ilemis is desperately fighting, and Aras doesn't hesitate either and stabs one crocodile. Eliah gestures him to draw back. At first Aras refuses but then he looks better into the depth, and he can see that everything is breaking down and monsters keep coming. Reluctantly they all start to retreat. Suddenly something emerges from behind the horizon of the celestial world, and they are also lit by a small light of hope. A huge army of the celestial creatures have come to support this defense and Eliah is both pleased and relieved. Ameris and Ardax are looking and a huge army behind them is waiting for their commands. The monsters notice this immediately and they are holding their positions. They are waiting for something that will redeem the dark creatures of the depths. Eld just grins as if he knew this moment would come. He blows the trumpet immediately and its sound is heard all over the horizon. Ardax exhales and realizes that the fun is just beginning. Ameris rolls her eyes and looks behind her, signaling everyone to get ready. Everyone turns their weapons into what suits them best in combat. Aras is breathing hard and preparing mentally for the coming wave.

Oliaf and Ilemis inadvertently rub against each other, and Ilemis smiles kindly at Oliaf. Oliaf sets up a harpoon as his weapon, which will shoot an infinite number of arrows, and Ilemis chooses the same one. Suddenly everything shakes, it starts to roll from the depths. The crocodiles in their positions are nervous and so are the masters who are leading them. Eld just smiles, looks into the depths, and feels the support of his coveted army. Suddenly, a huge hatchery of monsters emerges from the depths, led by Lex and Et and Rehat. The boulders like cover fire accompany those spooky vermin. Even the huge boas are hissing insidiously and quickly rolling to the wall of the net. Eld calmly joins the army, where he finds his favorite shark. Ardax just raises his hand to keep the army calm and waiting for his order to fire on the insidious enemy. A huge army of death is rolling towards the celestial world, which will now face a great test. The boulders hit the walls and create a massive cloud of dust through which nothing can be seen. Ardax is still holding his hand up and waiting, staring into the darkness, and feeling the threat they are about to face. The whole army is tense as it is waiting in that silence while the dust is settling. And suddenly the hand is down, signaling the army to start shooting. As the dust is settling, the army is mercilessly rolling with the shields organized in the lines. They are rolling to enjoy the bloody battle. The celestial army is shooting like crazy, and a lot of predators die hit by the celestial shots. However, still a lot of them survive the attack and they are almost face to face to their enemy. Eld is excited and he is encouraging the bloodthirsty army to advance. Suddenly, the army encounters the first line of the celestial warriors. Eliah's army begins suffering, there is blood everywhere and it's almost impossible to see what's going on. Eliah and his fellow warriors are fighting fiercely, killing one predator after another. Another line of the celestial warriors joins them and it's a real pleasure to fight in that chaos. There is blood everywhere and the limbs are flying all around. Oliaf and Ilemis are fighting like hell, they've turned their weapons into the swords. Ardax and Ameris join them, being attacked by all different kinds of vermin. A lot of celestial beings are killed. For a moment, Ardax looks at the crowd of his warriors and he can see hopelessness because the predators are prevailing. The celestial army is taken aback that its defense is failing and also their armors are ineffective. "We didn't see this coming. But Ameris had to know, or she had a hunch that this might happen," thinks Ardax while fighting the monsters that keep attacking. Eliah signs Oliaf and Aras to take Ilemis away immediately. She doesn't yet understand what is going on and she is already pulled away by her guards even against her will.

Ameris nods her head at Eliah, who looks into the depths among the warriors and spots Eld. Eld notices Eliah, who looks deep into his eyes filled with enormous hatred. Eld, in turn, instructs Lex to pursue the refugees. He nods his head at Et and Rehat and tells them to divide the army attacking on the sharks. Ameris summons a group of Harasets, led by Retiana, to take Ardax to safety at once. Not wanting to risk the death of her love, she summons Achas's golden army of Karions to join the defense of the position. Eld, with help of his protectors, is going after Eliah, who is just waiting for him to come to him on his shark. They are striking back, and Eliah is still patiently waiting in his place with his numerous warriors protecting him. When they finally meet, both sides have their protectors. "It's been a while..." says Eld, longing for revenge. Eliah grins: "I've been waiting for this moment for so long." "Perfect. As usual, just you and me, nobody else, fight to death." Eliah nods: "Deal." "Bring it on then." "Oh, I will..." says Eliah, he takes out his weapon and turns it into a huge sword.

Ameris can see from the distance that the duel between Eld and Eliah is about to start but she has other things to worry about. Oliaf, Ilemis, Aras and Harasets are rushing up into the safety. Ilemis's vision is blurry but she knows that her father is going to fight against Eld but there is nothing she can do about it; she is already too far away. Eld jumps down off his shark and his weapons – the spear and smaller sword are ready. They are circling around each other in a combat position for a while and suddenly Eld attacks with a combination of spear attack and cut of a sword. Eliah covers up this attack. Their protectors are also fighting against each other to prevent anyone from interrupting the duel. Eld is attempting to attack Eliah again, but he keeps resisting. Then they pull away from each other and Eld is having fun. "I can see you haven't changed a bit." "I could say the same about you but one thing I know for sure: I won't make the same mistake again." Eld smiles. "What mistake exactly are you talking about?" Eliah suddenly launches forward and attacks Eld. Eld covers the first blow, which hits him near his waist. Then Eliah cuts swiftly towards Eld's head. The attack is successful, Eliah - very unexpectedly - cuts off Eld's head. Eld is dead in the blink of an eye. "This is the mistake I've been talking about." Eld's head is slowly floating here and there, his body is falling down. The blood is flowing all around, the entire army is standing still, and Lex turns around and he feels that his father is already dead. He screams: „no, no, no...." in his mind. Everyone is taken aback, just Ameris doesn't hesitate a moment and tells the golden army to continue suppressing the predators. There is chaos and the predators don't know what to do. Some of them start retreating, the other keep ransacking the place. Eliah immediately rushes up before they kill also Eld's protectors. The parts of their bodies are floating everywhere around. Ameris stops Eliah. "Eliah, just go to the world we've been talking about. Promise me you'll protect my brother Arbatron and my beloved Ardax and his family and friends." Eliah is looking at her surprisingly when suddenly giant snakes emerge, they wrap around Ameris and pull her into the depths. Eliah and others are trying to set her free. They manage to cut off a few snake parts, but Ameris is plunging into the depths helplessly. Eliah screams to her in his mind: "I promise I will protect everyone on the country of the celestial creatures." Ameris smiles faintly, shows thumbs up and vanishes in the darkness of the depths. Eliah continues swimming up while the golden army is pursuing the predators, driving them away where they've come from. A lot of blood is flowing all over the battlefield, not to mention the pieces of bodies that are flying here and there. The sharks, crocodiles and other monsters are escaping into the depths.

The celestial creatures are swimming very quickly. Retiana is urging everyone to hurry up. Her pace is incredibly fast and her fellow female warriors riding the dolphins are struggling to keep up with her. They are approaching the kingdom of Cetefs where the entire celestial kingdom is hiding but not for long because they all need to hurry, the waters of the celestial kingdom aren't safe anymore. Ameris has secretly built up a new territory where the power of the celestial world will grow stronger. However, the predators already know about the new shelter of the celestial creatures, they've even tried to get there in the different groups. Thanks to the safety nets, the celestial creatures were able to eliminate the predators. Furthermore, the predators can't adapt to this environment as well as the celestial beings. Those are much more adaptable in the new environment. Suddenly there is a beautiful fortress right in front of them. It is guarded only by a small group of the guards whose firearms are ready in case the predators win. However, these weapons won't be enough. The celestial warriors are coming after the battle which hasn't ended up well for either army. Retiana has made herself a trumpet and now she blows it to signal the arrival of the celestial company. The immediate panic arises, nobody knows what to do and they are swimming to and fro. Retiana arrives with her army and other allies. Her task is to protect everyone and get them into safety. She shouts in her mind: "Open up, you cowards!" The gate opens quickly and loudly and Retiana shakes her head. Her companions are staring as well, unable to believe their own eyes. Everyone's panicking, just a small group from Ardax's kingdom is quietly swimming up to them. Of course, they can also see Xetis's worried face and Ilemis is already preparing the reassuring speech. Xetis swims up to them like a huge tsunami wave and immediately asks the unpleasant question, let alone other creatures who are gathering in front of the gates. "Where is my beloved Ardax?" is the question which is so hard to answer. Suddenly they can hear a trumpet, and Ilemis feels huge relief. And they all look into the distance, where a small group of Assads and another accompanying army, led by only one leader, Ardax, appear. They are coming as fast as they possibly can, they are in a hurry. They are already at the gates, where everyone who has been waiting for the instructions from someone who knows where they are going has gathered. All celestial kingdom is awaiting with tension the words of Ardax and his brother Eliah who is desperately looking at everyone. There is infinite sadness in his eyes. He hugs her daughter Ilemis warmly when Ardax says: "Dear friends, I truly wish I had the good news. But I don't. This battle has been very bloody and murderous. I supposed this might happen, but we mustn't give up. But I have one piece of good news. There is a newly built world which will become our haven for some time and our nation will have an opportunity to develop. We have neither won nor lost this battle, but these waters aren't safe anymore. Our protective barrier is falling apart, and our entire defense will have to retreat and get into our new world. Please, calm down and follow Retiana and others. Just keep the line clean so that we won't kill each other. There is not enough time for useless questions because each delay might cost us our lives. We are already in danger because somewhere here there is a small group of predators lurking. We saw them when Ilemis and others were escaping. So, let's go to a new world!"

After Ardax's motivational speech they all gather obediently and set out on a journey to the new world. They are following Retiana and her group. They are passing right below the surface of the sea which is rippling beautifully. They can hear the waves crashing onto the shore of an island. They all put on the masks that provide them with what they need – water. They are spellbound by the beauty of the surroundings. They have never seen anything like this before. Their eyesight is only adapting to the new conditions, their vision is very blurred, but they are getting used to the environment when they are coming to the vast peninsula. Everything is green, there are trees everywhere. They are astonished by all those sounds because they have never known such a variety. There are some sounds under the water too, but it is much more different here, much nicer, and more colorful. They are slowly coming out onto the sandy soil which strokes their feet, they are diving their feet deeper into the sand to enjoy that beautiful feeling which is welcoming them to this new world. Everyone is on the land now. Only Ilemis and Oliaf are in the back, holding their hands and Eliah is looking at them with a smile on his face, they remind him of two lovebirds that have just fallen for each other. Oliaf turns back for a moment, and he sees that beauty. It's a lovely sight, the giant shiny ball is setting down beyond the horizon, everything is so glittery and so close. He stretches his arm as if he would like to touch that glow and it looks like he is really doing that... Even the horizon is somehow imperfect, but wonderful.

Ilemis is pulling Oliaf by his hand and urges him to keep going when suddenly something emerges from under the surface. A giant monster stabs Oliaf in the stomach with a spear. The monster is Lex Ion and even though he is extremely near to death himself, he is looking into Oliaf's eyes. He is losing his breath, but Et and Rehat draw him down under the surface and vanish in the depths of the ocean. Eliah and his fellow warriors react promptly, they are trying to catch the predators but those are long gone. Oliaf is staring into the space, and he can hear Ilemis scream with an echo: „No, no, no!" His stomach is bleeding and soon he is coughing out green blood. Ilemis hugs him around his waist, and she is pulling him onto the land. A big group of creatures gather around them, trying to help somehow, but it's too late. Ilemis puts down his mask to say goodbye to him. She looks into his bloody eyes. "Oliaf, Oliaf.." she says crying and her voice is trembling. These are the first words of the sea creatures, and they are the words of sadness. All of them put down their masks and breathe in the fresh air. It takes some time to get used to but soon they are breathing normally. As autotrophic beings they can adapt fast. Oliaf just smiles a little and says in a weak hoarse voice: "Don't worry, Ilemis. Look at all that beauty around. Enjoy this wonderful place. I love you." Oliaf's breath died with the last word that made Ilemis cry and shout. They tried to calm her down, but everything was in vain. She hugged him so hard, she couldn't let him go, she cried over the unfulfilled love that tormented her immensely, as if she wanted to go back to all those moments and change everything. But it is not possible. With a broken heart at this moment, Ilemis swears that the cruel predators will pay for it all, in the sea world they already controlled.

The world is shrouded in darkness, and Ardax and everyone else are watching with astonishment at the beautiful interplay of lights in the heavens. Everything was so close that darkness was not darkness but a beautifully lit world with multicolored objects in the heavens, which celestial creatures had yet to get to know. They can hear the marvelous sound of the sea and it only beautifies the view of the heavens. At that moment, other celestial creatures appear and speak to them in a strange language.

"Easy, easy, we are coming in peace. Welcome to your new home. My name is Arbatron."

Peter Kent

The Legend of the Stones of Life

(The birth of the Gods)